GALILEE

D.L. TRACEY

authorHOUSE®

AuthorHouse™
1663 Liberty Drive
Bloomington, IN 47403
www.authorhouse.com
Phone: 833-262-8899

Published by AuthorHouse 02/17/2021

ISBN: 978-1-6655-1730-0 (sc)
ISBN: 978-1-6655-1728-7 (hc)
ISBN: 978-1-6655-1729-4 (e)

Library of Congress Control Number: 2021903313

Print information available on the last page.

Any people depicted in stock imagery provided by Getty Images are models, and such images are being used for illustrative purposes only.
Certain stock imagery © Getty Images.

This book is printed on acid-free paper.

CONTENTS

The Loss of My Grandchild

The first son of my son arrived the other day,
brother and sister born hand in hand.
Oh...what a wonderful bond.
Who would have known
two would be forever torn apart?
When Liam said goodbye to his sister, Keira,
after a few brief moments of togetherness,
who would have known
they would be forever torn apart?
The pain in my heart, the tears in my soul are forever.
I will never get to babble silly baby talk,
get a smile or two,
or croon the sleepy lullabies
I wanted to sing to you.
I wanted to rock you in my rocking chair,
rock you to and fro.
Grandfather's arms are not meant to be empty.
From the day your dad grew up and went away,
I waited and waited for this day, but not this day.
I waited for my first baseball game with you,
I waited to hold your hand as you took mine,
I waited for our first story together as you climbed into bed,
I waited for your first step and your first leap.
If my love could have saved you, you would have lived forever.
Liam, I will stop missing you...when I am with you.

Grand Dad

CHAPTER 1
The Arrival

New England Winters are well known for their bone-numbing winds whipping off the Atlantic Ocean like a cold, razor-sharp knife ripping through outer clothing, cutting quickly to the bone marrow. New England winter storms are known for their wicked drops in temperatures to well below freezing in the blink of an eye. It gets so cold you can taste the icy freeze as you labor to breathe in. And this cold February morning was no exception to any of these basic New England winter rules. The warmth from the cab heater never quite made its way through the smoke-stained plastic partition to the back seat, making the hour-long cab ride seem even longer and much colder to the young priest.

"Fifty-eight eight-five, Father," the cabbie yelled in a typical thick Irish Boston accent, bringing the old yellow station-wagon-gone-cab to a bumpy, sliding halt on the slush-covered gravel road overlooking Point Judith Bay. The cab ride from T.F. Green Airport in Providence to the small fishing port of Galilee, located in the coastal town of Narragansett, Rhode Island, had been a long, tiring ride in the early-morning hours.

Looking out the frost-crusted and yellowing, smoke-stained windows of the cab, the priest could barely make out anything except the Point Judith lighthouse as it swung its beacon of light out to sea in the misty distance of the awakening gray sky. "Hey, Father, fifty-eight eighty-five," the cabbie yelled again in a hoarse voice over the crackling blare of an early-morning radio talk show, which, the priest thought, was turned up as loud as it could go.

Fumbling for his wallet, the priest yelled back over the blare of the radio, "Where is the church?"

The cabbie, never quite turning around to face the priest, nodded through a thick cloud of bad-smelling cigar smoke at a small stand of trees and bushes off to the right. The priest turned to look at his new home. After a moment, the church of Saint Peter came into his view as if on cue, the swirling snow came to a rest.

Built in the mid-1800s, the small church was made of red brick, with a black slate roof to withstand the harsh winters and the frequent nor'easters that swept in off the Atlantic Ocean like runaway trains smashing into the coast all winter long. The church was first used as a school and parish poorhouse. Sundays and Christian holidays, it was used as a church. Sometime around 1900, the school was closed, and a full-time parish was established.

Not what I was hoping for, the priest thought. Seven very long years of seminary school, top of his class in every course. What had the archdiocese placement board been thinking when they'd assigned him here? Opening the door of the cab, the priest was greeted by a stinging hello, a howling gust of wind. It tore his black umbrella from his grasp, sending it on a bumpy ride down the slush-covered street. "Damm," mumbled the priest, stuffing three twenty-dollar bills into the plastic bill slot in the cab partition window. He yelled to the cabbie above the howling wind and radio noise, "You can keep the change."

Climbing out of the cab, the priest was once again greeted by a gust of stinging wind. This time, he could taste the salt on his lips, and it stung his eyes. Raising his arm for some protection from the driving wind, he chased his wayward umbrella as it bumped down the street. Finally, it came to an abrupt halt, lodging itself in a pile of slush and dirt on the side of the road. As the priest neared it, the stinging wind howled and threatened to take it once again on a bumpy ride further down the slush-covered street.

Lunging for the wayward umbrella, the priest lost his footing on the slippery gravel street and fell with a loud *thud* on top of the umbrella, crushing it beneath him. His glasses fell off in the fall, and pulling himself to his knees, the priest retrieved them from a pool of slush. Wiping the slush from them, the priest put the water-streaked glasses back on.

Looking off to his left, through the swirling snow and rain, the priest could just make out a small, gray-haired man in a black overcoat standing in front of an old wall made of rocks, with a metal gate at the end farthest from the church. Hands in his pockets, a gray scarf hanging around his neck, swaying slightly in the wind, the old man had a slight smile on his face as he shook his head in amusement. *That must be Father Gilday*, thought the young priest. *Great first impression*. As he struggled to stand, he waved to the old man. Just then, he heard a car door slam.

Turning, the young priest watched as the yellow cab drove away. His two old black suitcases had been left in the middle of the slush-covered street. *Mental note to self*, the priest thought. *Never use that cab company again*. Turning, the priest noticed the old man had vanished. *Must have gone back inside the church, where it is warm. Guess he had enough of the Father Hickey Show for one day*. Picking up his umbrella, the priest went to retrieve his two suitcases, filled with all his worldly possessions.

Retrieving them, the priest awkwardly dragged them towards the walkway of his new home. Suddenly a mother cat and three kittens scurried across his path, their tails up in the air, and the disappeared into the stand of trees to his left. "Well, at least they were not black cats," the priest said with a slight smile. The walkway had been shoveled in the last hour, it seemed to the priest, and the fresh rock salt crunched under his feet as he walked toward the church.

The cold ocean breeze off the Atlantic stung his nostrils as he fought for the breath he'd lost from his less-than-graceful fall. The early-morning glare of the rising sun, made worse by the reflective snow, made seeing while walking almost impossible, so much so that he almost walked into a statue in the middle of the church walkway.

It was almost too late when he more sensed than saw something in front of him. Stopping abruptly and dropping his suitcases, he shielded his eyes from the glare of the morning sun. Taking a moment to let his sight adjust, he scanned the statue. After a moment, he immediately knew who the statue was.

"Poor Saint Peter," the priest said. He smiled just a bit. Saint Peter had tried to walk on water and had fallen in. Surely, Jesus had a sense of humor in making Simon Peter the saint of all fishermen. "Kind of like sending me here to this crappy little outpost of the church," the priest said to the statue of Saint Peter. "Yes, but you, Saint Peter, are now the gatekeeper of Heaven."

What was the hierarchy thinking? I spent seven very long years in the seminary. Took every scholastic honor they had at the seminary school and then some. All that hard work just to be assigned here to this parish, the priest thought as he continued to examine the statue of the saint.

The young priest was quickly brought back to reality by another group of five or six cats in various colors passing in front of the statue. Picking up his suitcases, he let out a reluctant sigh, and then he continued his slow, slippery journey on the church walkway. *I hope the cats know where we are going,* he thought as he followed the cats around the side and to the back of the church.

Off in the distance, the sound of wood being chopped broke the morning silence, echoing through the crisp morning air like static electricity. Still following the parade of slow-moving cats on the ice-covered walkway, the priest approached a snow-covered porch that he hoped led to the living quarters.

The smell of burning wood filled the cold morning air. "Hope there are two bedrooms in there," the priest said to a group of three calico cats sitting lazily on the porch railing, enjoying the early-morning sunshine. His mind started to wander back to the early years at the seminary, to his first roommate, Paul Lang, who snored so loudly due to some sort of nasal condition that if the young priest did not get to sleep first, there was no rest that night due to the non-stop sound of logs being sawed.

Then his mind wandered to his later years at the seminary and the late nights with his roommate Father Ward, a much older priest who had a very bad drinking problem. Sometimes, after one of his many long drinking stints, Father Ward would come back to the room. Getting naked, he would try to climb into bed with the young priest. *How many times did I have to fight that man off?*

A seagull screaming in the distance brought the priest back to reality. Shaking off the memories of Father Ward and some very bad nights, he stomped his feet on the wooden porch to get the slush off his shoes. On the porch were two very old rocking chairs, one on each side of a wood stove that gave off a warm glow and the sweet smell of burning wood inside of it.

"Hope there are two bedrooms," the priest said again to the two lazy cats as they climb onto the rocking chairs to be near the warmth of the stove.

Knocking on the door, the priest took a step back. Looking off to his right, he noticed that behind the old rock wall he had seen earlier was a small graveyard with maybe twelve or so grave markers in it. In the middle was a small white granite bench with a worn marble cross standing behind it. *For mourners to sit and pray, no doubt*, the priest thought. In the far-left corner of the graveyard, there appeared to be a fresh grave with no marker yet. Next to the new grave was a large pile of brush and stones partially covered by crusted snow.

Beyond the graveyard, Point Judith came into view in the early-morning light. Looking out over the bay, the priest watched as the small fishing fleet headed out to sea for a long, cold day of fishing. The sound of the Point Judith ferry horn screamed loudly in the distance as the ferryboat left for its first trip of the day to Block Island, just a few miles off the coast of Rhode Island.

CHAPTER 2

---✛---

"May I help you, sir?" a female voice with a thick Polish accent said from behind. As the startled priest turned, almost tripping over his two bags, he came face to face with a small older woman standing slightly back in the entrance, trying not to leave the warmth of the house. Once again, the old woman said, "May I help you, sir?"

Gathering his composer from his near fall, the young priest said as he untangled himself from his luggage, "Yes, yes, my name is Father Hickey. May I speak with Father Gilday, please?"

With a startled look, the women stepped back and motioned for him to come inside. "Oh, Father Hickey, we were excepting you a few days ago. Please, Father, come in." Picking up his bags, the priest stepped inside.

"My name is Maria Szymanowska. I am the housekeeper here." She motioned for the young priest to come further into the room. "Please wait here, Father Hickey, and I will get my husband. He speaks better English than me." Grabbing a jacket and pushing past the priest, the woman hurried outside to find her husband, leaving Father Hickey to survey the room.

There must be a church rummage sale going on here today, the priest thought. The room was littered with half-packed boxes, and clothes were piled on tables and furniture all around the room. Over in the far corner, closest to what appeared to be the entrance to the kitchen, a small television sat on a chest of drawers. Many pictures hung on the far wall. An old, checkered couch, a wooden rocking chair, two swag lamps, and a few small tables rounded out the furnishings.

The sound of frantic footsteps crushing the snow outside brought the priest's attention to the door. He watched as a giant of a man clad in a heavy gray wool parka entered from the porch, followed by his wife.

The man stretched out a huge hand. "Good morning. My name is Jedrek Szymanowska," he said in a thick Polish accent as he pulled back the hood of his parka with his other hand. "My wife, Maria, and I are the caretakers of this parish. The young priest reluctantly took the offered hand. "Father Gilday expected you three days ago. The giant shook the hand of the young priest, almost crushing it in his grasp.

"Yes, I know," replied Father Hickey as he struggled to get his hand back from the giant's grip. "The plane from Kansas ran into some bad weather, and that caused a few delays." He thought back to the two-day stop in Chicago and sleeping in the airport terminal. The seminary had given him just enough traveling money for food and the plane ticket to Wichita, Kansas, for a family visit and then back to his first parish here in Rhode Island.

"Well," the giant man said, "we have some bad news for you. Father Gilday passed away four days ago." Tears came to his eyes as his voice broke down. He looked to his wife for comfort in his pain, and she came over and held his hand. "Father James from the Providence Archdiocese came down and did the burial services yesterday. He asked that you call him as soon as you get here."

"Yes, of course. Where is the phone?" Father Hickey replied, still reeling from the news of Father Gilday's death.

"It is right over here in Father Gilday's office," Maria said, gesturing to a door in the back corner of the room.

Father Gilday's office was small and cluttered, with books overflowing the bookshelves that lined the wall and in piles on the floor and stacked near the couch. There was an old black leather easy chair in front of a fireplace. A small fire in the fireplace warmed the room. "Father Gilday heard confessions in here," Jedrek said half to himself and half to Father Hickey as he handed over a slip of paper with a phone number on it. "Guess this is your office now." With a sigh, he pointed to a phone on the old oak desk that sat in the corner of the room. There were two windows on one side of the room, facing the graveyard.

Sitting down in the large leather chair behind the desk, Father Hickey reached for the phone. Mrs. Szymanowska walked in from the kitchen with a steaming cup of black coffee and the local morning paper. "Father Gilday liked his coffee with the paper to read in here every morning."

"I like my coffee with cream and sugar," Father Hickey said, trying to return the cup.

"Yes, but Father Gilday liked it this way. As black as my robe, he would say. That is how I like my coffee." She hurriedly walked back to the kitchen.

"I guess I will drink it black," Father Hickey mumbled to himself as he started to dial the rotary phone.

The call was quick and to the point. Someone from the archdiocese would be down before week's end. With another major nor'easter hitting the coast of New England this week, it would not be wise to travel until it had passed. So, Father Hickey should just sit tight and do his job as he was trained. If he had any questions, he should just ask Mr. or Mrs. Szymanowska; they knew the routine of the congregation well and could be a big help. Hanging up the phone, Father Hickey said to the room. "Great. Now what am I supposed to do?"

The giant man was standing quietly just outside the office door, waiting for the young priest to finish his phone call. "Excuse me, Father. My wife and I are heading home now. Will you need anything else today?"

"Home?" Father Hickey said with a puzzled look on his face.

"Yes, my wife and I come three times a week to clean the church and take care of the grounds. If it snows, I will come and shovel the walks one hour before mass. Will you need anything else today?"

"No, I suppose not, but I am not sure what I am supposed to do here."

"Well," the giant man replied, "Father Gilday had mass every day at nine, heard confessions on Thursday, and blessed the fishing fleet every Saturday morning at six. Our phone number is in the Rolodex on the desk. My wife does your shopping on Monday for the week. The keys to the church car are in the top drawer of the desk. You can sleep in Father Gilday's room. My wife has changed the sheets and cleared out both closets and dresser drawers. I guess it is your room now."

The realization of what the giant had just said slowly sank in.

"We will be back early tomorrow to tend to the grounds and clean the church. My wife will finish packing Father Gilday's things then. Do you need anything else, Father Hickey?"

"No thank you. I will call you if I have any questions," the priest replied, and then he mumbled to himself, "Guess I'll just sit and wait for the archdiocese to drag their lazy asses down here later this week to show me around."

"Sorry that you have walked into a mess here, Father Hickey, but you were picked to be here for a reason. Hopefully, it all becomes clear sooner rather than later," the giant man said as his wife pulled his arm, signaling she was ready to leave.

"Thank you very much, Mr. Szymanowska," the young priest replied, looking up from the desk.

"Please, Father Hickey, just call me Jedrek." With that, the giant and his wife turned and left the room.

Sitting at his new old desk, Father Hickey took a long, hard drink of the hot coffee and choked back the twigs-and-stick taste of the charred blend. *Aggg, this stuff sucks, but it is hot, he thought*. Twisting in the chair, he looked out the window. "What a view I have," he said. As he gazed out over the salt marshes, the Atlantic Ocean came into view. A few boats could be seen dotting the calm sea.

The laugher of a young child caught the young priest's attention. Swiveling around in his chair, out another window, he saw a little girl kneeling in the snow. The child was all wrapped up in a bright red jacket, long yellow scarf, and bright red cap. Next to the child was an older woman dressed almost the same as the child. *Must be the mother*, the priest thought.

The mother and child were laying some flowers on a small grave right under the window. They started to walk away, but then the little girl turned and ran back to the window, the snow crunching under her bright yellow boots. With bright red cheeks, she smiled and waved at the priest. The mother yelled, "Come on, Emma. We need to go now." The priest smiled and gave a halfhearted wave as the little girl turned and ran to her mothers' side. Turning, the little girl looked back at the grave and waved, and then she and her mother walked through the iron gate, which clanged loudly as the mother slammed it shut.

The sound of a door slamming shut startled the priest. Looking out the window, he saw the giant man and his wife climbing into a pickup truck parked off to the side of the church. Hearing a dog bark, Father Hickey turned his attention back to the graveyard. Running back and forth inside the gate was a small white dog with a black splotch on it. *Well*, thought Father Hickey, *this is way too noisy for this time of the day*. Getting up from his chair, he grabbed his jacket and headed outside.

9

CHAPTER 3

✢

Upon opening the door, Father Hickey was once again greeted by a howling, salt-soaked wind, and bright morning sunshine. Grabbing hold of the porch rail, he started down the steps towards the graveyard gate. The wall to the graveyard was made of stone and mortar and was about four feet high. *A little too high, I guess, for the dog to jump over*, he thought as he approached the gate. Opening it, he called, "Here, dog. Here, dog. C'mon, boy, let's go. Time for you to leave. Go home." However, the only reply was the howl of the icy, salt-soaked wind.

"Where did you get off to, puppy?" Father Hickey wondered aloud. The priest walked slowly into the graveyard. The snowed-covered gravel path led to the small, weathered granite bench. The marble cross behind the bench was old and graying from years of New England weather. Some words were chiseled on the cross. Wiping away the thin crust of ice, Father Hickey mumbled to himself, "Sit tibi terra levitas. Hmmm, written in Latin. Let's see. 'May the earth rest lightly on you.' No name on the cross, guess it's just for show."

Walking to his left on the fresh morning snow, the priest passed a few small gravestones. Near the end of the row, the priest found a small wooden white cross underneath his office window. On the small cross was a single word, "Jackie," written in black paint. Next to the cross was a small wicker basket with a few dog bones, a blanket, and a red rubber ball in it. *This is where the little girl was standing*, the priest thought. "Cute, now I also run a pet cemetery," he said with a slight smile.

As he turned away from the small cross, Father Hickey almost tripped over a black slanted gravestone about knee high. "Damm!" Kneeling, he wiped away the thin crust snow that had gathered on the face of the gravestone. An etched picture of a child's teddy bear on one side came into view as the snow fell away. As the priest continued clearing the snow, he quietly read, "To the child who rests here known only to God, may the love you lacked in life now be rewarded in Heaven. You are remembered." As the last of the snow fell away underneath the words, a small bronze nameplate came into view. Stamped on it was: "Boy 2002."

"Ouch," Father Hickey said to the howling wind. "Poor child, never knowing what life could have been. What a cold, lonely place to rest for all eternity. Well, you are with your Father now." He made the sign of the cross in the air above the stone. Wiping away a tear, he rose to his feet and scanned the graveyard once again for the little dog.

Behind the marble cross, he found a tall white grave marker with a crucifix carved into the stone face. Pulling his jacket tighter around his neck to ward off the howling wind, the priest walked over to the marker: "Father Thomas Tarmey, born Jan. 15, 1848, died March 20, 1932."

"Tarmey. Ahh, yes, the first priest of this parish," Father Hickey muttered to himself, remembering the fact sheet he had been given on the day he'd been assigned here. "Well, Father Tarmey, any advice on how to survive my cold stint here in the parish of Saint Peter?" he asked the gravestone.

A seagull perched on the marble cross cried in reply. Turning his head, Father Hickey shielded his eyes from the glaring sun. He saw the silhouette of a man in a long coat and with his hands shoved deep in his pocket, looking down at a gravestone. The priest moved slightly to his right, so the glare of the sun was blocked by the cross. "Sorry to startle you," the man said with an outstretched hand. "My name is Ted Roberts."

"Ted, nice to meet you," the priest replied, stepping forward to shake the man's hand. "My name is Father Hickey. I have been assigned here to work with Father Gilday."

"Bit of a chill out today, Father. Yes, very sad about Father Gilday. He died a few days ago. He was a good friend of my mother's until she passed away last year. Sad, very sad," Ted said in a voice that trailed away as he looked down at his mother's grave again.

His mother or Father Gilday? the priest wondered. "Well, Ted, your mother is at peace now. She is with God and Father Gilday," he said in a comforting voice.

"I do not sense she is at peace," the man retorted in a low, angry tone. "That woman was never at peace. Well, it was a pleasure to meet you, Father, but I must get to work now."

"Same, Ted. If you ever feel the need to talk, I am here."

"Thanks, Father, but that will not be necessary." Ted turned and strode briskly away from the priest, the fresh snow swirling about him as he walked towards a car parked in front of the church.

Well, that was weird, the priest thought.

Turning his attention back to the dog hunt, he decided it was time he gave up. *Well, he must have gotten past me*, he thought as the cold wind started to chill him. Shivering, he hurried back to the gate. Passing a grave, he looked down and quickly read the white stone tablet: "Mark Hansen, born June 1932. Died Sept. 1999. Beloved Husband and Friend. Rest in Peace." *Bit cold for resting today*, the father thought. Grabbing hold of the gate, the young priest gave it a good push to open it further. "I will leave the gate open, dog," he yelled to the hiding dog in the graveyard. Moving his hand from the gate, he noticed a word carved into the top.

As he squinted in the early-morning sun, the word came into focus. "Gehenna. Well, that is some sort of mean joke," he said as he reached out and touched the word. *Why would anyone take the time to etch this into this metal?* he wondered as he rubbed the cold, wet word to see if it could come off. Looking down, the young priest kicked a pile of snow into the gate to keep it open in case the dog was still in the graveyard.

Hunched over to avoid the stinging wind, Father Hickey continued his hurried trek to the church porch. Snow crunched underneath his shoes as he tried not to slip, and he raised his hand to shield his eyes from the glare of the sun as it reflected off the morning snow. Stepping onto the porch, the priest stomped his shoes briskly to clean off the snow and ice. *Better buy some warm boots*, the priest said to himself, looking down at his wet shoes.

Turning back to look one more time for the dog, Father Hickey saw three people: a man, a small child playing in the snow, and an old lady standing in the graveyard, looking at the cross. "Busy day for mourners," he said to the chilling wind as it howled around him. Opening the door to the warmth of the church quarters and quickly stepping inside, he shut the door quickly behind him. Hanging his coat on a wooden peg next to the door, he realized he had yet to see his new church from the inside.

The door to the main church hall was to the left of where he had hung his coat. An old, rusted latch held the door shut. When he opened the door, three black and gray cats came scurrying past his legs and disappeared into the living area of the home. "Damn," he muttered. "How many cats live here?"

He stepped into the main room of the church. "Man, it is cold in here," he quipped to no one as he watched his breath float away in the cold morning air. Kneeling in front of the small wooden altar, he prayed in silence for a moment for the small child, a life cut short, buried in his graveyard.

Making the sign of the cross, the priest rose, turned, and scanned the inside of the church. "Hmm," he mumbled, counting to himself. "Two rows with five pews in each row times five people per pew makes a fifty-person church," he said in a dejected voice. Fifty people. Walking between the rows of wooden pews, the young priest thought how foolish he'd been to hope for a huge parish in Boston or even New York to speak to a service of thousands of Catholics at one time.

Realizing that he had come to the end of the dark aisle, the young priest looked up to see the early-morning sun streaming in through a stained-glass window as his breath rose in the cold air. The large window covered most of this side of the church. "The Good Shepherd," he mumbled. The glass window depicted our Lord as the one who saves and rescues those who are lost. "Jesus is pictured as the Shepherd, with the lost lamb in one arm and a crook in the other, the instrument of rescue. I sure could use a rescue from here," he said to the stained-glass window.

Looking to his left, the front entrance of the church came into view: two large black wooden doors with grated, see-through windows near the tops. A thick rope dangled from the ceiling near the right door. "BONG, BONG, BONG," went to the church bell as the priest yanked on the rope. *Whoah, better not do that again. Next thing you know, someone will be getting a ticket for making too much noise in this crazy village.*

As he walked back down the aisle to the living quarters, the phone rang in the office. Quickening his pace, he made it to the phone on the third ring. "Saint Peter's Church. May I help you," he almost yelled into the phone.

"Yes," came a startled voice. "Is Father Gilday there?"

"No, Father Gilday passed away a few days ago. This is Father Hickey, his replacement. May I help you?"

"Yes," came back the voice. "This is Officer Mark Luke of the Galilee Harbor Patrol. We have the fishing trawler the *Imogene* coming into port with a crewmember needing last rites. Can you help us out, Father Hickey?"

"Of course, of course," the priest replied, "but this is my first day, and I have no idea how to get anywhere yet."

"That's fine, Father. I am sending a car for you right now. It should be there in fifteen minutes. Please be ready."

"Fine, I will be ready," the priest replied as the phone hung up. *Wow, not too friendly*, he thought.

Ok, where is my cassock? Which bag did I pack it in? Ahh, here it is. He pulled the long black robe out of his luggage. *Could use an iron right now, but I must hurry.* As he shook the garment out, doubt started to enter his head. Yes, he knew last sacraments, but he had never given them to any dying person or tried to comfort them in their last moments on earth, and if there was family, then what? Pulling on the robe, he reached for the worn leather Bible on the desk. As he reached back into his bag and pulled out a small wooden box, a car horn sounded outside the church. "Man, that was a quick fifteen," the priest said to the door.

Grabbing his jacket, the priest stuffed the wooden box into his jacket pocket. On his way out the door, he almost tripped over a group of four cats huddled against it for warmth. They all tumbled into the house, scattering in four different directions before the priest could do anything. The horn sounded again as he pulled the door shut. Pulling his jacket tight around his neck, he ran, or more like shuffled, along the iced walkway to the waiting car.

He climbed in as the car started to move. "Excuse me! Can I get all the way in before we head for the races," he said in a sarcastic voice.

"Sorry, Father, my orders were to get you to the docks ASAP," the young driver replied.

"The key words are 'getting me there,' soldier," the priest yelled above the roar of the car as they sped away from the church.

"Seaman First Class Hill," thundered the reply from the front seat as the car slid through a hard turn, and then the driver hit the gas once again.

"So, do you know what the situation is?" the priest yelled above the roar of the racing motor.

"No, sir, my orders are just getting you to the dock. That is all I know. C.O. McNally will meet you there and will fill you in on what needs to be done. Those are my orders, sir."

Looking through the glass windshield in the front of the car, Father Hickey could see the seaport of Galilee coming into view. Off in the distance, the mast and rigging of the fishing vessels slowly filled the sky above the town.

As the car slowed for a stop sign, the priest noticed to his left a large, round wooden sign" "Welcome to the Port of Galilee." Behind the sign was a stone structure about two stories tall and twenty feet wide that came to a point at the top.

"What is that building for?" the priest yelled, pointing to the stone building off to their left.

As the driver hit the gas, he called back, "Oh, all the names of men and women who have died at sea from this port are chiseled on the granite walls inside. That is the Galilee Fisherman Memorial."

After a moment, the driver called out over the roar of the car engine, "We are now in Galilee."

CHAPTER 4

As the car slowed, small buildings and storefronts started to dot the side of the small road into the fishing port: Bay State Fish Company, Bob's Fish Trap, The Bait Shop, Bay Ice Company, Ocean State Quahog Company. "Every building has to do with fish and the sea," the priest said.

"Well, yeah, this is a fishing port," the driver sarcastically replied.

Ignoring the remark, the priest called back, "Are we almost there?"

"Yes, sir," came the crisp reply. "Just up ahead, sir. And here we are, sir," the young man called out as he pulled the auto to an abrupt stop.

A small group of people surrounded an ambulance at the top of the dock where the car had stopped. Climbing out of the car, the sailor ran around and opened the door for the priest. "Here we are, Father." As he got out of the car, Father Hickey was assaulted by the smell of rotting fish and the salty, cold air. "The tall man in blue over there is the C.O. He will answer any questions you may have." The cries of seagulls filled the air, and a boat horn echoed in the distance. Looking to his left, the father noticed a bar; the sign said, "The Crow's Nest."

A group of men and women standing on the second-floor balcony were smoking and chatting amongst themselves as they looked down on the ambulance. *The experts are out today*, the priest thought. *People love to watch someone else's misfortune, always glad it's not them. Heck, I'm always glad it's not me.*

"Excuse me, are you Father Gilday?" a voice said off to his left.

"No, sorry, Father Gilday passed away a few days ago." The priest turned to see a man in blue. "You must be Mr. McNally."

"Yes, sir, C.O. McNally. And you are?"

"Oh, I am Father Hickey. I was supposed to be Father Gilday's assistant. Now I am not so sure what will be happening."

"Well, either way, Father, I am sorry to rush you down here." Turning back towards the crowd, C.O. McNally yelled, "Make a hole!" As the crowd moved aside, the C.O. ushered the priest towards the ambulance. "Early this morning, the Coast Guard received a distress call from the fishing boat *Imogene*. Said they were bringing in a hurt crewmember who needed last rites. Turns out he died about a week ago. Fell off the boat and was caught in the dragger net for the better part of the day before anyone thought of bringing it up to see if that was where he was." They stopped at the back of the ambulance.

"Why did the captain of the *Imogene* wait so long to bring the body back to port?" the priest asked in a puzzled tone.

"Same exact question I put to him," the C.O. said. "The captain says to me, 'Hey, the guy is dead. Was I supposed to miss making my fish quota to bring him back early?' So, they just put him in the fish hold, wrapped in a tarp, and packed him in ice for the ride home. Father, you must understand, this is how they make their living around here. No fish, no money. It might not be my way, but it is their way."

He looked over at the small group of people. "But Father, the family tells me they still want you to give the body last rites. The remains are in the ambulance if you feel up to it." Turning his gaze to the ambulance, the man in blue continued. "But I gotta tell you, Father, twelve hours stuck in a net being dragged on the ocean bottom and a week laying with dead fish in ice hasn't been too pleasant to the remains."

"No, this is why I am here. This is my job," Father Hickey said as he started to walk towards the ambulance. Stopping at the ambulance door, the priest took off his jacket and gave it to C.O. McNally. "Oh, the wooden box in the pocket, can you give it to me?"

"The wooden box?" the C.O. replied, removing the box from the jacket.

"Yes, it holds my sanctified oils to perform the sacrament of last rites." The priest nodded to the attendant to open the ambulance door.

As he climbed into the dimly lit ambulance, the young priest started to feel the death he was about to see. The smell of rotting fish and flesh filled the cold air. The smooth black body bag lay strapped on the stretcher in the middle of the cabin. A small pool of water was growing on the floor as the body thawed.

The attendant climbed into the ambulance. "Ready, Father?" he asked as he reached for the big brass zipper ring on the bag.

"Yes," replied the priest in a weak voice as he began to shake from the cold or nerves. *Which is it?* the priest wondered as he watched the ambulance attendant grasp the brass ring.

In one quick motion, the attendant unzipped the black body bag. A strong, rancid smell escaped into the air, and the priest and attendant gagged. Trying to regain some of his composure, the priest moved back towards the open body bag. It took everything he had to hold down last night's dinner. Gagging for breath, the attendant moved quickly past the priest and left the ambulance for the cold, fresh ocean air.

The time in the ocean and the fishing hold had not been kind to the body. *What an understatement*, the priest thought. The face was frozen in agony, like the poor soul had known he was dying and there was nothing he could do. The skin was transparent, like the old see-through models the priest had seen as a kid of the human body in science class. But the priest knew this was no science model. The skin had changed into a slimy, jelly-like substance. The priest could feel nausea coming over him again as water started to seep out of what was left of the eyes of the dead fisherman.

"Easy, lad," said a gentle but firm voice from behind him as a bear-like hand lay gently but firmly on his left shoulder. Turning his head, he could barely make out the silhouette of a large man. The afternoon sun shone over the man's shoulder, partially blinding the priest. "Excuse me?" the priest replied, squinting in the bright sunlight.

"Get on with your job, Father, so this poor soul can get on with his final journey," the big hand man said, nodding towards the body on the stretcher. "Get on with your business."

Nodding in agreement, Father Hickey turned back towards the body. Taking the Bible out of his pocket, he opened it and placed it on the body's chest. He took the wooden box from his other pocket, opened it, and set it on the floor next to the body. Then he removed a small vial of holy oil from the box and began the last rites. "Through this holy anointing, may the Lord in his love and mercy help you with the grace of the Holy Spirit."

Taking the holy oil, the priest poured a small amount on his hand. Then he made the sign of the cross on the forehead of the body with the holy oil.

"Through this holy anointing, may the Lord pardon you whatever sins or faults you have committed in this life. May God be with you." As he closed the Bible, Father Hickey could feel the nausea returning once again.

The attendant pushed past him and pulled the zipper closed, covering the body in its black shroud once again. "Damm, it took long enough. That smell was killing me," he said as he moved past the priest and out of the ambulance.

Gathering his Bible and holy oil, the priest headed for the ambulance door. Climbing out of the back of the ambulance, Father Hickey was greeted by the big bear's hand again. As the father stretched out his hand, the big man said in his Irish accent, "Afternoon, Father. My name is Michael McDonough. I own the Crow's Nest over there." He nodded in the direction of the bar. "Sorry, Father, I was a bit rough on you in there, but you seemed like you were about to lose it, and that would never do."

"No, thank you. It was just the focus I needed at the time. You are right – I was about to lose my dinner at that point," Father Hickey said, smiling back and holding out his hand.

"Sorry to hear about Father Gilday. He was a great man and will be missed at church and the Crow's Nest," the bear-man said with a bit of a sad laugh. "And he was truly a good friend," he added half aloud but mainly to himself. "Well, come on. You must be hungry, Father, and I am sure, since it is afternoon now, you could use a spot of whiskey to ward of the cold and settle the nerves after that." The bear-man nodded at the ambulance as it drove away.

"Not a point I need to argue," the priest said, and he followed the bear-man up the steps and through the door into the smoky barroom.

"Come, let's sit here," the big man said, motioning to a chair, which he pulled back from the table. "Hey, Jimmy, bring us two glasses and a bottle of Old Comber. Also, tell Janie the new priest is here and to bring us out two of her finest corned beef and cabbage lunches."

"Right away, Mike, a firm Irish voice echoed back.

"Here, have a seat," came the offer again.

Sitting down, Father Hickey could feel the chill in his bones as the excitement of what had just happened started to wear off.

"Quite a start to your first day here in Galilee, Father."

"Yes, yes, it was. I think I have had about all I need today."

"Here we go, Mike," the bartender said, setting the bottle of whiskey and two shot glasses on the table.

"Ahh, thanks, Jimmy lad. Oh, Father Hickey, this is Jimmy. He works here as one of the bartenders."

Reaching out, Father Hickey shook Jimmy's hand.

"Rough day for you out there, Father?"

"A bit, but I pulled through it thanks to Mike here. Calmed me down just when I needed it."

"Yeah, Mike is a real archangel, he is," Jimmy said as he headed back to the bar, laughing a bit on the way.

Pouring two shots, the big bear-man handed one to the priest. "Well, here's to Father Gilday. May the road rise to meet you; may the wind be always at your back and the sunshine warm upon your face, May the rain fall softly upon your fields, and until we meet again, may God hold you in the hollow of his hand. Cheers."

As he threw back the whiskey, Father Hickey could feel the warmth of the smooth liquid fill his body and take away the chill of the morning.

"So, what do you think of Galilee, Father? What is your first name, anyway?"

"Tommy," said the father, trying to hold back the warm liquid, which now did not want to stay with him.

"Tommy, yes, that is a good name for a priest," replied the bear-man. "Well, Tommy, what do you think of our little seaport?"

"To be honest with you, I never heard of it until last week when I got assigned here."

"Wow, bet this came as a surprise."

"Yes, you could say that," the priest replied.

"Let me give you a bit of the history around here, maybe give it a little face and character," the bear-man said, pouring another shot for himself and the priest.

CHAPTER 5

"In 1902, the story goes, Thomas Mann, an angler from Nova Scotia who had settled here, felt the village that had sprung up with its fishing shacks should be called Galilee, after the fishing village of biblical times. One day, an old-timer sat on the docks, repairing his nets, when a stranger called out to him, 'Where am I.' The answer was, 'Galilee.' 'And what is that?' the stranger asked, pointing to the other side of the channel. The old-timer thought for a minute, nodded, and replied, 'Must be Jerusalem.' Now, there is much more to the history here, but I always enjoyed that version myself. Gives the port a bit of color. Now, as for that church of yours, the parish of Saint Peter, there is quite a tale indeed to its history."

"Here ya go, Michael. Two corned beef and cabbage dinners," said a woman with a thick Irish accent.

"Thank you, Janie, thank you. I want you to meet Tommy. He is taking over for Father Gilday."

"Well, pleased to meet you, Father Tommy."

"No, please, just Tommy," said the priest. "My last name is Hickey."

"Well, please to meet you, Father Hickey, and welcome to the Crow's Nest. Sorry about Father Gilday. He was a good man and a regular for the corned beef and cabbage. Well, back to work. Pleased to meet you again." She quickly headed back to the kitchen.

The young priest twisted in his chair as he watched her go. When he turned back to the table, he was confronted by another shot of whiskey. "Yes, she is easy on the eyes, that is for sure," the bear-man said with a smile.

"Excuse me?" the priest said, trying to act innocent.

"Ahh, man first, priest second, I always say," the big bear-man said with a smile and a nod to the kitchen. "She has worked here for seven years now. Does not talk much to folks, though she did like to sit and talk with Gilday from time to time. Well, eat up while it's hot. Best corned beef and cabbage this side of South Boston, most folks around here always say."

Tossing back the shot of whiskey, the bear-man started his story again. "The parish of Saint Peter was part of a national experiment in social welfare reform. If memory serves me correctly, and it always does," he said with a smile, "the Catholic Church started some programs to help the less fortunate. They started poorhouses and farms around the country. The parish of Saint Peter was one they started here in Rhode Island around the summer of 1832. They gave it a Latin name meaning 'saved by hope.'"

"*Spe Salvi*," the priest said as he sipped his drink.

"Yes, that's it. How did you know that?" the bear-man asked.

"Well, it seems I have a knack for speaking dead languages—six, to be exact."

"Wow, six," said the bear-man.

"Yes, I am what you would call an overachiever in dead languages."

"That's weird. Father Gilday spoke four. Well, anyways, the social experiment never worked. For years, the parish poorhouse and farm were viewed as a destination of no return for the insane, the tubercular, and the just plain poor. According to urban legend, no one ever left there. Around 1900, the experiment was considered a failure, and the insane were shipped off to Woonsocket and Boston hospitals. The poor were just shown the door. The farm was torn down, as well as many of the houses and buildings, but the church was left, some say on orders from the Vatican."

"What about the small graveyard next to the church?" Father Hickey asked.

"Excuse me, Father, came a voice from the door of the bar. Turning, the priest saw the man who had driven him there from the church. "Will you need a ride back to the church, sir?"

The response rang out above the noise in the bar before the priest could answer. "I will drive him back," Janie said, walking over to the table. "I will be off soon, and I am going that way anyway, so if it is ok with you, Father, I would be happy to give you a lift."

"Sure, if it is no problem," the priest replied.

"No," Janie replied. "Just a few things to do in the kitchen, and I'll be all set to drive you back to the church." Turning briskly, she walked back to the kitchen.

After pouring another drink of the Irish whiskey into the priest's glass, the bear-man continued with his story. "The graveyard? Not sure when it began. It seems that when the poor and insane started to die, they were just buried around the farm and the church with no real rhyme or reason. No one can be sure where all the graves are up there. No markers and no real records except for the site next to the church. Father Gilday had the wall erected about fifty years ago."

"He was here fifty years?" the priest said.

"Yes, this was Father Gilday's first and only parish," the bear-man said sadly, reflecting on the years gone by and the loss of a dear friend.

"Wow, you think I will be stuck here for fifty years like him?" the young priest said in a dejected tone.

"Stuck here? Why would you say that? I thought being a priest meant going where you were needed. Well, Tommy, trust me; you are needed here in Galilee."

Feeling the warming effects of the whiskey, the priest shot back, "Seven years of study. I was top in every class. Graduated with every honor there was."

"Ready to go back to the church now, Tommy?" Janie said, yelling above the noise from the front of the bar.

"Thanks for the food, Mike."

"It's just the whiskey talking, Father. Do not worry. I am sure God sent you here for a damn good reason."

"Well, let us hope so," the young priest said, and he held out his hand, shook the bear-man's big paw goodbye, and headed for the door and his waiting ride back to the church.

He stepped outside the bar and into the below-freezing New England afternoon. "Father, over here," Janie called. Squinting in the bright sunlight, the father saw Janie climbing into a beat-up blue pickup truck across the street. "Come on," she yelled to the priest. "You will catch the death of cold."

Pulling his jacket collar tightly around his neck to ward off the cold, the father headed across the street to the waiting truck. Looking out the window of the bar, the bear-man watched as the young priest made his way to the truck and climbed in. "Kids," he said to the window. "Well, time will tell. It always does." He took a long drink from his glass, watching as the truck slowly pulled away from the curb and headed down the street.

"So, Tommy, did you know Father Gilday?" Janie yelled above the roar of the radio and a muffler that had a few too many holes in it.

"No, I heard his name for the first-time last week when I was assigned here."

"Where are you from, anyway, Father?"

"Born and raised in Kansas. And you?"

"Oh, nowhere, really," Janie said in a quiet tone.

"Everybody is from somewhere, Janie," the priest said, looking out the window as the town slowly went by. "Where is your family from?"

"Not sure," Janie replied. "Most of my life was spent in foster homes and a few bad marriages. Do you mind if I smoke?" Not waiting for a reply, she lit a cigarette.

"You know that smoking will kill you?"

"Yeah, so I have heard. But then again, what won't kill you these days, Father? So, why did you become a priest?"

"Excuse me?"

"You heard me, Tommy. Why did you become a priest?" she asked again.

"Well, I am not sure. I just knew it was always for me."

"A calling from God, anything like that?" Janie said as she slowed the truck for the stop sign at the fisherman's memorial.

"No, I guess, for as long as I can remember, all I ever wanted to do with my life was a priest. You know, help folks with their sins and stuff," he said with a meek smile. "And you, do you like being a cook?"

"Nope, but it pays the bills," Janie called back above the blare of the radio as she blew smoke out the half-open window of the truck.

"Hurry up!" Janie yelled at a car going through the intersection. "Come on, grandma, this isn't no parade! Wow, some folks just cannot drive in this weather."

"So, did you know Father Gilday long, Janie?" the priest asked.

"Yes, going on six or seven years now. I met him when I first moved here. Went to church one morning to ask God for some help, and there was Father Gilday. We have been friends ever since. Now Father Gilday is gone." She started to cry.

"Well, I am here now, so maybe we can pick up our friendship where you left yours with Father Gilday. True, I do not have his wisdom. However, I do listen well, and that is always a good start in this line of the business," the priest said with a reassuring smile.

"Thank you, Father. I will give your offer some thought. Here we are." Janie pulled the truck to a sliding halt in front of the church.

"Thanks, Janie, and the offer still stands. Anytime you need to talk, I am here for you," the young priest said as he climbed out of the truck.

He shut the door, and with a nod of her head, Janie drove off, splashing the priest with muddy ice water as she gunned the motor to get out of the deep slush.

Stepping back from the spray, the priest said, "Damm, I just had this jacket cleaned." Mumbling to himself and the salty wind, he struggled to wipe the slush from his face. As he walked slowly towards the church, he contemplated the first day of his first assignment. *Thought I would get some sort of orientation day to start. Never thought I would be thrown right into the trenches.* Laughing, the priest continued up the pathway to the church.

Off in the distance, Father Hickey could hear the ferry horn boom out to announce its arrival into port. As he walked around the church, more cats appeared in front of him. "Ok, ok, you cannot all live here. Or can you?" he said to the group of five or so cats looking at him. Looking out at the sea, the priest could see the moon rising from the ocean. His watch said it was 5:15. The sun was already leaving for the day, and the moon was going to work.

Feeling the whiskey's effects, the priest headed for the church's living quarters with quite a few cats in tow. "I hope I did not lock the door," he said to the cats. *I did not take the keys with me*, the priest thought. Stepping on the porch, he heard the dog barking again. Looking out at the graveyard, he could not see the dog, only hear its bark. *Well, I am not looking again.* He noticed that the gate to the graveyard was still open. "You can leave when you want to! The gate is open, silly dog!" he yelled.

He tried the door, but as he feared, it was locked. *Damm, now what am I going to do? Break a window? Maybe the main church door at the front is open.* As he turned and started down the stairs, he looked up at the sky.

The sun was almost gone now, and storm clouds seemed to be touching the sea as they moved towards the coast. He could feel the temperature dropping as the cold settled in for a long night, and he picked up his pace.

As he walked past the statue of Saint Peter, the priest stopped for a moment. *Not a bad life this fisherman led. Met the savior of all mankind and was called by many to be the first pope of the Catholic Church, the church God Himself asked Peter to build, according to Matthew 16:18.* The priest said to the statue. "And I tell you, you are Peter, and on this rock, I will build my church, and the gates of hell shall not prevail against it."

Peter, the fisherman, was there when this all started. "Not a bad life at all, he said to the statue before continuing the trek to the front door of the church.

CHAPTER 6

✜

The front doors to the church groaned open as the priest pulled the handles. "Finally, a break," he said in triumph. As he stepped inside the dark church, a few of the cats followed him in. When he closed the door behind him, the icy wind helped push it shut with a bang that echoed throughout the church.

He took a moment to catch his breath and adjust his eyesight. The dim glow from the candles flickering at the front of the church was the only light in the church now. *So, where are the light switches?* he thought, fumbling around the wall by the door. After a moment, he mumbled to himself, "Not here. Better make sure I ask the bear-man where they are. He could have shown me today if he hadn't been in such a hurry to get home. Oh, well. Let's see if I can find my way to the back."

Blessing himself with holy water from the small font on the wall, Father Hickey grabbed the top of the first pew to his right and started walking slowly in the dim light towards the back of the church. It was very cold in the church. *Hope there is heat in this pace*, he thought as he reached for the second pew. Coming into view in the dim light above the altar was the hanging cross with Jesus on it. The light from the Point Judith lighthouse came through the window behind him, lighting the whole church for just an instant. Off to his left, he thought he saw someone sitting in the first-row pew, wearing a black jacket and with gray hair.

"Hello. Can I help you with anything?" he called out in the direction of the figure. Taking a few more steps, the priest called out again, "Is anyone here?" The light shone through the window again, and he scanned the pews for the visitor. There was no one there now. *Wow, guess I had a bit too much Irish whiskey to drink at the bar today. And that poor soul at the dock today. It's no wonder I am seeing things. I must be tired.*

Kneeling at the altar, Father Hickey said an Irish prayer his grandmother Agnes had taught him as a young child. "May He support us all day long, until the shadows lengthen, and the evening comes, and the busy world is hushed, and the fever of life is over, and our work is done. Then, in Your mercy, Lord, grant us a safe lodging and a holy rest and peace at the last with You. AMEN."

Well, Agnes, I made it. I am now a priest, and I have my own parish already. Not what we hoped for, but here we start. He thought back to his younger days and the grandmother who raised him for many years when no one else would even give him the time of day. His parents had been too busy with their own lives to bother with his, so a small Irish woman on his dad's side had taken him off the street and given him the power of God and all the goodness that came with it. To repay this woman for her kindness in giving him a chance at life, he joined the priesthood. It was a shame Aggie had died two years ago. She would have been proud of her little one, as she called him. Standing back up, Father Hickey felt his stomach growl. Whether it was from the whiskey or the corned beef, he was not sure; he just knew he was hungry again. *Well, let's see what we have in the kitchen to eat,* he thought as he turned to the door to the living quarters.

From the shadows, as he watched the young priest walk through the door, the old man in black shook his head and turned back to his prayer.

Upon flipping the light switch in the kitchen, Father Hickey realized that this was the first time he had been in this room. By most standards, it seemed to be a modern kitchen with a double-door refrigerator, gas stove, microwave, dishwasher, coffee machine that was already set up for 7:00 a.m. the next day, a small, round table with four chairs, bright yellow walls, white tile floor, and green trim. A double window provided a great view of the ocean, and the lights of fishing boats blinked in the distance.

"I really hope Mrs. Szymanowska stocked up some great stuff," he said, opening the refrigerator doors. "Bingo," he said with a smile. Inside was a case of Coke, bottled water, a few different juices, milk, cold cuts, Sam Adams beer, and a wrapped plate of fried chicken with a date on it in tape indicating it would be good for three more days. "Jackpot," he said, grabbing the chicken and beer from the refrigerator and shutting the door with a kick of his foot.

"Well, let's see how this chicken tastes." As a child, he'd always loved his grandmother's fried chicken. It had always been a big deal, going every Sunday to his grandparents for fried chicken with the rest of the cousins from the Hickey side of the family. Sometimes, with the adults, there were over twenty people there, he thought with a smile. Then his grandpa died, and the fun in the weekly gatherings' kind of lost steam as his grandma took to drinking after the loss for the next few years. *Hmm, it was good chicken, though.* He sank his teeth into the first bite. *Cold and crunchy is the best*, he thought as he took a drink of his beer to wash down the chicken.

Looking around the kitchen, he noticed a small television in the corner next to the stove. The remote was on the table. "Well, let's see what's on tonight," he said, hitting the on button. "Local news. Ugh." He flipped through the channels. "Well, at least there is cable," he said to the wrestling show that had just come on.

As he stared out the window, thinking of what had happened on his first day here, the priest was startled to hear the phone ring. Looking at the clock above the stove, he was surprised by the time. *Wow, seven o'clock already.* Just then, the phone rang again in the office. Grabbing the beer and a fried chicken leg, Father Hickey made his way through the cluttered living room and into the office, picking up the phone on its fifth ring.

"Hello, Saint Peter's Parish," he said into the phone.

"Hey, big brother, where you been?" It was Father Hickey's little brother, Paul. "So, you don't call and let us know you made it," he said in a voice only a little brother can throw at you.

"Hey, dummy. No, I got here this morning, and it has been very hectic since I arrived. Father Gilday, the priest I was supposed to be working with, passed away a few days ago."

"Man, that sucks," said his little brother in a true dumb-little-brother tone.

"True, Paul, this does suck, but it has been busy since I got here. I did last rites for a fisherman this afternoon. Then I had a few drinks and corned beef at the local pub with a big Irish guy who goes by the name of Michael McDonough. Quite a guy. Grandma would have loved him. Looks like a big bear.

Well, Grandma only would have loved him if he were a big Irish bear," Paul said, chuckling over the phone.

"Isn't that the truth," said the priest, nodding in agreement.

"So, how is the weather there in Rhode Island these days?"

"Cold, real cold, and it looks like a storm coming in off the ocean," the priest said. Leaning back in his chair, he looked out the office window at the light from Point Judith lighthouse as it cut through the falling snow and came into view over the water. His gaze followed the light as it swung over the graveyard, and the priest thought he saw a little spotted dog running out the gate.

"Finally, he is gone."

"What?" asked his little brother.

"Nothing. A dog outside is finally gone. It's been here most of the day, barking non-stop."

"Hey, I gotta go now, big brother. Don't be stupid. Call occasionally and let us know you're alive."

"Sure, Paul. You know me," the priest said with a smile." I will talk to you later. Bye."

"Bye," was the response back, followed by the click as his little brother hung up.

Hanging up the phone, Father Hickey sat back in his chair again and looked out the window at the graveyard for a moment. It had started snowing quite heavily in the last hour or so, and the wind was whipping the fresh snow all around, so even seeing the cross in the graveyard was getting hard. It was getting a bit late, so maybe it was a good time for bed. *Ahh, my first night in Rhode Island*, he thought as he stood up from his desk and walked to his bedroom.

He had been in the room earlier but had been rushed to get ready for the ride into town, so he really hadn't had the chance to scope it out. In the room were two beds separated by a nightstand with a lamp, alarm clock, and clock radio. To the left of the closet was a bathroom with a shower stall. There were two tall dressers against the wall and a small desk with a chair in the corner.

Near the window was a rocking chair. The window looked out over a large field, covered with snow right now, with the ocean as a backdrop. Off in the distance, he could see the lights of the Galilee fishing fleet in port, getting ready for their next day of fishing. A large, old orange and white cat walked into the room and started to rub up against his leg. "Hey, cat. Bit too cold for you outside tonight," he said, taking another swig from his beer. "Well, you can stay in here tonight." Father Hickey opened the closet and saw that all his clothes had been hung up and put away.

Mrs. Szymanowska must have come back and hung them up for me. I must remember to thank her for that, he said to himself as he grabbed some sweatpants and a sweatshirt to sleep in. While changing, he could hear cats fighting outside, somewhere off in the field. "Man, let's hope this doesn't go on all night," he said to the window as he looked outside to see if he could see where the cats were. Finishing the last of the beer, Father Hickey turned the radio on to a news station to break the silence that comes with sleeping by yourself. Kneeling next to the bed, the priest bowed his head and began his nightly prayers.

"Only begotten Word of the Father, Jesus Christ, who alone are perfect, according to the greatness of your mercy, do not abandon me, your servant, but ever rest in my heart. O Sweet Jesus, Good Shepherd of Your flock, deliver me from the attacks of the enemy. Do not allow me to become the prey of Satan's evil intent, even though I have within me the seed of eternal damnation. Instead, O Lord, Jesus Christ, Adorable God, Holy King, while I sleep, protect me by Your Holy Spirit, through Whom You sanctified Your Apostles. Enlighten my mind by the light of the Holy Gospel, my soul by the love of Your Cross, my heart by the purity of Your teaching. Protect my body by Your sacred passion, my senses by Your humility, and awaken me in due time for Your glorification. For You, above all, are adorable, together with your Eternal Father and the Holy Spirit, now and ever and forever. Amen."

Shutting off the light, Father Hickey climbed into bed, rolled over, and quickly fell into a deep sleep. The large, old orange cat sitting on the window frame growled softly at the night outside the window.

CHAPTER 7

The sound of shoveling woke Father Hickey from his deep sleep. The early-morning sun was starting to make its way through the bedroom drapes. The radio was talking about the local news: temperatures below freezing for the rest of the week and more snow expected. According to the radio, over a foot of snow had fallen during the night. The local police were investigating several cat deaths over the night in Galilee. At last count, fifty-five cats had been found dead. Many of the cats were strays, but many more were the pets of local owners. Authorities were blaming the bad weather and a pack of coyotes that had been seen in the area, looking for food.

The clock read 7:15 a.m. Well, time to get up, I guess. Too much noise to get back to sleep, Father Hickey said. Hitting the off button, he got up and slowly walked out into the kitchen, nursing the hangover from his drinking the night before.

The rich, hickory aroma of fresh coffee filled the kitchen. The local paper was on the table, along with the morning mail. Pouring a cup of coffee, Father Hickey sat down at the table and started to look over the mail. A knock on the kitchen door startled him, and he turned to see Mr. Szymanowska, the giant man, covered in snow, his face barely visible in the fur-lined hood covering his head and face. He held an old wooden shovel in his gloved hand.

Waving, the priest said, "Please come in, come in."

As the bear-man opened the door, a rush of cold salty air and snow swirled into the kitchen. "Good morning, Father Hickey," the giant said, stepping into the kitchen and quickly slamming the door shut. Shaking off the cold and snow like a giant dog, the giant pulled back his hood and shook his head again. "The walkway is clear, and I cleaned up the cats and covered the blood."

"Excuse me?" the priest said.

"Yes, I cleaned the walkways."

"No, I understand that Mr. Szymanowska. The cats that lived around and inside the church?"

"Yes, there were about thirty dead cats around the church when I got here this morning to shovel, so I picked them up and will take them to the dump on my way home. I covered their blood with snow as best as I could."

"Thirty cats?"

"Yes, Father, around thirty."

"How did they die?" the priest asked as he tasted his coffee.

"Not sure, but it happens all over the port. The news said it was a coyote pack. I don't think so, though. Coyotes kill to eat. Someone just killed these cats to kill them, for the sport of it." The giant looked out the door to his truck. "Well, Father, do not forget, you have service in a little over one hour. I will see you then, after I take the dead cats to the dump." Pulling his hood back on, the giant turned and walked out the door, shutting it behind him.

"Thirty cats," the priest said. Could it have been that dog he'd heard barking yesterday? *No, I doubt it*, he thought. It was not a big dog that he saw leaving the graveyard last night, and thirty cats would take some doing. Sipping his coffee, it finally dawned on him what the giant had said: *I will be back for mass in one hour. Mass, one hour. Damn. Now what?*

The young priest had done mass many times but never by himself. A few times, he had led mass but only under the strict supervision of one of his teachers. He had never really written a sermon and certainly had not written one in an hour. "Well, this is going to be one of those days. I can just feel it now," Father Hickey said to the old cat. "Bet you are glad you were inside last night," he added as it rubbed up against his leg.

He got up from the table, and as he was pouring himself another cup of coffee, he heard some noise in the church, and he went inside to see what was happing. Two young boys were cleaning the pews and placing Bibles in each row. All the lights were on and lying across the front pews were two altar boy gowns. "Good morning, boys," he said, bringing the two young men to attention. "My name is Father Hickey. I am here to work with Father Gilday."

"He passed away, sir," the bigger boy said. Behind him, the smaller was not moving, just trying to stay out of sight of the new priest.

"Yes, I know Father Gilday passed away a few days ago," the priest replied, trying to see the younger child. "But that just means that, for now, I will have to wing it. I could sure use your help, as I am new here and just out of school. So, I will need all the help I can get." The two boys just continued to look quietly at the priest. "Hey, I know, he said. "I will be the altar boy, and you two can do the mass for me, ok?" The two boys smiled and then laughed.

"Sure, Father, we are just kids," the small one said, stepping out from behind the bigger boy.

"Well, to my mother, I am just a kid, too, so let's see if us kids can get the job done today. I will need lots of help, as this will be my first solo mass."

"Ahh, it's easy," said the bigger boy. "Father Gilday showed us everything."

"Great. Let's get started, then," Father Hickey said with a smile as he sipped his coffee. "So, you guys have names?"

"Yes, Father, of course we do," the little one said, laughing.

"Great, so what are they? Or do I just call you Tom and Jerry?"

"No, Father," the big one said. "My name is Ricky, and this is my little brother, Glenn."

"Well, Ricky and Glenn, I am Father Thomas Hickey. So, how old are you two?"

"I am ten, and Glenn is eight," Ricky said.

"Where do we start, guys?" the priest asked.

"Well," Ricky said, "we set up the church already."

"Set the church up?"

"Yes," chipped in Glenn. "We cleaned the pews, lit the candles, and put out the Bibles. And if Mr. Szymanowska doesn't shovel, we do it. But he always does the shoveling."

"Don't you guys have school today?" the priest asked.

"No," said Ricky, "it's February vacation, so we get to do mass during the week. When we have school, we just do mass on Sunday."

"Ok, then," Father Hickey said, "does anyone know where my vestment robes are?"

"Yes, Father," Glenn said. "They are in the closet over there." He pointed to a door to the right of the altar.

"Thank you, Glenn," the priest said, and he walked over to the closet.

Opening the door, he found four robes in various colors of red, violet, white, and green. Turning, he saw Ricky looking into the closet. "What do the colors mean?" the boy asked.

"Well, Ricky, this red vestment represents blood."

"Blood?" said Glenn, joining the conversation.

"Yes, but it is worn when celebrating the events of Jesus's Passion and the feast for the martyrs of the Church. Violet signifies preparation and anticipation. It is worn during the times of Advent and Easter. White is the symbol of purity and is worn during very happy occasions and celebrations, like Christmas. Green, well, that is the color of life and growth and can be worn almost anytime you feel in the mood, I guess."

"What shall I wear today?" the priest asked. "Let's try the white robe. Today is my first solo mass, and it is going to be a celebration. Well," he added with a worried look, "let's hope so. All right, guys, I am going to get ready, and come get me when it is time to start the service.

Father Hickey headed for the living quarters with the white vestment robe in hand. "Sure thing, Father Hickey," Ricky called out as the priest left the church.

I am not ready for this. Father Hickey headed into the office to gather his rosary and Bible. *What a beautiful day*, he thought as he looked out the office window. The air was so clear he could see the town of Jerusalem across Point Judith Harbor. The morning ferry was on its way out of the harbor, to Block Island, a few fishing boats dotted the harbor entrance, and the air was alive with seagulls fishing around the mouth of the entrance.

As he took a sip of his coffee, the priest noticed some people in the graveyard. One appeared to be Janie, the cook from the Crow's Nest who had given him a ride home the day before. Kneeling, she laid a flower at the child's grave, and she appeared to be crying. Ted Roberts, the man he'd met yesterday in the graveyard, was also there. *Paying respects to his mother again*, the priest thought. Over in the back corner of the graveyard, at the pile of stones and brush, was a woman so bundled up against the cold he could barely make out it was a woman.

Taking down her jacket hood, he saw the long brown hair and pale complexion of a lady in her mid-forties. She stood there for another moment. Then, spitting at the pile, she walked briskly towards the church.

Janie was now joined by the big bear-man from the bar, Michael McDonough. Putting his hand on her shoulder, she rose to stand next to him. Looking up at the window, she abruptly turned her head away when she saw the priest watching them. The big man took her by the arm, and they started to slowly walk towards the church.

"Father Hickey, we are ready," came a voice from the office door.

Turning, the priest saw Glenn, dressed in his altar boy robe and smiling. "Well, don't you look spiffy in your robe? So, did anyone show up for mass today, Glenn?" the priest asked with a smile.

Laughing, Glenn said, "Yes, Father Hickey, people show up every day for mass. The church is always full. Ricky said we are ready, Father."

"Wow, full every day?"

"Yes, Father. Ricky said we are ready," Glenn said again with a smile.

"Ok, I will be there in just a minute. Let me just pull my robe on."

"Sure, Father," Glenn replied. "You're the boss here." He turned and headed back towards the church.

Father Hickey smiled to himself and shook his head. *If my friends could see me now.* Pulling the robe over his head, he headed for the church. Stopping at the door to straighten his robe, he thought, *Well, here goes nothing.* He blessed himself, and clutching his Bible tight for strength, he opened the door and walked slowly into the church.

The parish was singing "Amazing Grace," and as Father Hickey made his to the altar, he noticed there was a full house for his first service. *Well, whadda ya know? Little Glenn was right.* Glancing over the crowd, he guessed that the church was full. Fifty people filled the pews, and a few men were standing by the wall near the main entrance. In the front row sat Janie, Mike the bear-man, and two men the priest had yet to meet. Behind them sat the giant man, Mr. Szymanowska, and his wife. *A packed church today*, Father Hickey thought with a slight smile. Walking up to the podium, he raised his hands, made the sign of the cross in the air, and began his first solo mass.

36

"In the name of the Father, and of the Son, and of the Holy Spirit," he said as he made the sign of the cross in the air once again.

"Amen," said the church crowd.

"As we prepare to celebrate the mystery of Christ's love, let us acknowledge our failures and ask the Lord for pardon and strength." Motioning with his hands, the priest said, "Please, all be seated. My friends, I ask your forgiveness today, as I have a few things that must be said before I continue with my first mass as a priest and my first mass here at the church of Saint Peter. My friends, from Solomon, the son of David, king of Israel, comes the wisdom of Proverbs 11:2. When pride cometh, then cometh shame: but with the lowly is wisdom."

Looking over the crowd, he could see many of the people recite the verse as he said it. He continued. "A famous football coach was on vacation with his family in Maine. When they walked into a movie theater and sat down, the handful of people there applauded. He thought to himself, *I can't believe it. People recognize me all the way up here.* Then a man came over to him and said, 'Thanks for coming. They will not start the movie for fewer than ten people. With you and your family here, we now have more than ten.'"

Laughter rose from the crowd. When it subsided, Father Hickey continued. "My friends, I came here feeling the same way yesterday. I felt I was too good, that I had worked too hard in school to end up in such a small parish. I felt betrayed. Today I have come to realize that this is not about me. It is about our God and the work that must be done. About being there when I am needed, like yesterday for the poor soul who needed help with his final journey to the glories of Heaven. I am saddened by my lack of compassion for the uncertainty of his journey."

As he looked down at the altar, tears welled in his eyes. "I am ashamed in front of my God and you people here today. I humbly beg your forgiveness, patience, and understanding." Looking back at the crowd, he could see all eyes were riveted on him. "Let us continue the mass." He made the sign of the cross. "In the name of the Father, and of the Son, and of the Holy Spirit."

CHAPTER 8

Tradition after mass is for the priest to stand at the entrance of the church and meet the parishioners as they leave the service. Standing at the front of the church today, Father Hickey hoped the reviews of the mass would not be too critical. He held his breath as the first parishioner approached.

"Father Hickey, that was quite a mass," an older man said as he held out his hand. "It would seem, Father, you have been taught a great lesson in humility on your first day here in Galilee."

"Thank you," the priest replied, taking the man's hand in a firm grip. "And you are?"

"Andrew is my name, Father. Well, it was a pleasure to meet you, Father Hickey. I will see you at tomorrow's mass, and once again, I enjoyed today's sermon a great deal."

"Thank you, Andrew," Father Hickey said as Andrew walked out the church door.

"Father Hickey," said the giant man and his wife, who were next to approach the priest, "that was quite a sermon." The bear pulled the priest's hand into his own hand, shook it a few times, and then let go.

"Father Gilday would have been very proud of you," his wife chipped in as she reached out and shook Father Hickey's hand.

"Thank you very much, Mrs. Szymanowska. That means very much to me. I am also grateful you could make it to my first mass."

"Oh, Father, we come to mass every day," said the giant man. "So, does everyone here. With the passing of Father Gilday, it has been a few days for all of us, so today was, indeed, a good day for a church service." He helped his wife put on her coat, and they started for the door. "Well, see you tomorrow, Father Hickey, and thanks again for a great service," said the giant man as he and his wife disappeared out the church door.

"Father Hickey, that was quite a sermon."

Turning, the priest again came to an outstretched hand. "Why, thank you very much, sir."

"Yes, it has been a few days since we have had a church service here in Galilee. We had to drive up to Newport the other day for service. But since the weather has been getting worse, we have not been able to go anywhere the last few days. So, you can imagine our thrill to hear a new priest had come to the church of Saint Peter." Just then, a lady nudged the man speaking and whispered something under her breath to him. "Oh, I am sorry," the man blurted out. "I have forgotten my manners. I am James, and this is Mary. Sorry, Father, just the excitement of your sermon today, I guess."

"Quite all right," Father Hickey replied in an understanding tone. "I was a bit excited myself, though more nervous, to be honest with you."

"Well, thanks again, Father," James said as he helped Mary put on her coat.

"We will see you again soon, and maybe meet for dinner sometime next week if it is all right with you," Mary blurted out as they started for the church door.

"I would like that very much," Father Hickey called out to her as she waved good-bye.

For the next ten minutes, Father Hickey chatted with the parishioners as they left the church. Finally, as the young priest turned to talk to the next person, he realized they had all gone. Looking down the aisle, he saw the bear-man and Janie still sitting in the front pew.

"Father Hickey," called Ricky from across the pews to the priest's left.

"Yes, Rick," he called back.

"Glenn and I will pick up the Bibles and see you tomorrow morning for services again."

"Great, Rick. You and Glenn are the best altar guys in the whole Catholic Church, I bet," Father Hickey said with a smile and a wave.

Blushing, Glenn said, "We will see you tomorrow morning, Father."

Turning back to the front of the church, Father Hickey had to step aside as Janie strode past him, her head down, without saying a word.

"Janie," he called to her as she stepped quickly out the door of the church. As he started to follow her, the big bear paw once again came to rest on his shoulder.

"Let her be, Tommy," the bear said softly. "Janie is not ready to talk to anyone just yet."

"It seems she needs someone to talk with right now," Father Hickey said.

"True enough. She had someone. Janie and Father Gilday talked all the time, sometimes for hours. Give her time, Tommy. Janie feels she just lost the only person she could really talk to. The bear looked back at the altar.

"When Janie first came to Galilee, no one knew her or where she came from. She just showed up one day at the Crow's Nest, asking for a job. Said she didn't want to be a waitress, just a cook. Told me she doesn't much like people and would be happy in the kitchen. No one still really knows her," the bear-man said half to himself and half to the priest. "But Father Gilday kept with it, and at some point, they became friends, and whatever was bothering her, he knew about it. So, Janie is taking Father Gilday's death extremely bad right now." Making the sign of the cross, the bear turned back to the priest. "Well, Tommy, off to work.

On his way to the door, the big bear-man stopped for a moment and called back to Father Hickey, "Why don't you come to the Crow's Nest for dinner, and we can talk some more?"

"Sure, Mike, I can do that, but no more of that Irish whiskey. It came at me a bit hard last night."

"Sure, Tommy, no Irish whiskey with dinner. Just Irish beer," the big man said with a smile. Turning once again to leave, he called out, "Bet you slept nice and warm though last night because of it. See you later, Father Hickey." He disappeared out the front door of the church, closing it with a bang behind him.

"Excuse me, Father, can I have a moment of your time?" said a slight voice from behind the priest.

Turning, the young priest almost fell over an older lady wrapped in a gray and white woolen parka. "Hello. Sure, how can I be of help to you today? Father Hickey held out his hand for the woman.

"Father, my name is Annemarie Hanson."

"Well, pleased to meet you, Miss Hanson."

"Oh, please, Father, just call me Annie. Everyone in Galilee calls me that. I wish you would also," Annie said with a smile as she pulled her hand back.

"Annie it is, then. So, how can I help you today, Annie?"

"Well, Father, I need you to clear up a question for me if you can."

"I will sure give it a try. Would you like to sit down? The priest motioned to a pew.

"Why, yes, Father. You are very kind." Annie took a seat in the pew. As the young priest sat down next to her, she continued. "Father, is it a sin to take your own life?" She started to cry.

"Well, Annie, the short answer is, yes, it is a mortal sin to take your own life. Why do you ask?" The young priest took the old lady's hand.

Crying even more, Annie continued. "I miss my husband, Mark, so much since he died. He was my first and only love. Since he has left me, I am so alone, so terribly alone. Mark came to me last night, saying he was so cold and alone. He pleaded with me to help him; told me it wasn't like we thought it would be. The cold ground, no warmth, no love, just the terrible cold and endless loneliness. No light, just terrible darkness. My Mark was a good man, Father Hickey. Where is our God? Why does he forsake my Mark?" The old woman sobbed as she clutched the priest's hand.

"Annie, the loss of a loved one is never easy. You had a terrible nightmare," the young priest said in a soothing tone as he put his hand on the old woman's shoulder.

"But Father, this was not a dream," Annie said desperately as she looked up at the priest. "I was not sleeping. I was awake and reading in my home when Mark walked in last night."

From Father Hickey's expression, the woman knew he did not believe her. "But it is true, Father Hickey. I am not some old fool."

"Never said you were, Annie. It's just that the pain you are feeling right now is very real. I do believe that you saw Mark last night, but Annie, our Lord would never let one of his children suffer so." The priest lifted her chin so he could look her in the eye. "Mark was a good man. He is truly with our Lord, Annie."

"Pray for my poor Mark," the old woman said as she looked back at the priest.

"Of course, Annie. It will be my privilege to pray for Mark." Grasping her hand tighter, the priest prayed, "Eternal rest, grant unto them, O Lord, and let perpetual light shine upon them. May the soul of Mark, the faithful departed, through the mercy of God, rest in peace. Amen."

"Thank you, Father. I am sorry to have bothered you."

"Annie, why did you ask me about taking your own life?" the young priest asked. He already knew the answer but needed to ask anyway.

"I am sorry. It is just that Mark is alone and so am I. Mark cannot come here, so I need to go to him. It seems such a waste to leave one while the Lord takes the other."

"Annie, it is because God needed Mark, I am sure. And you, my dear lady, I am sure you are still needed here." The priest helped the woman to her feet.

"Yes, Father, I am sure you are right."

"Annie, I am sure it was just a dream, a very bad dream. But I am here anytime you need me. Please do see me if this happens again," the priest said as he opened the door to the church.

The path was well salted, and Annie took the priest's arm and walked with him towards her car. "I am sorry to have bothered you with the rants of a silly old woman, Father." She pulled her keys from inside her jacket. "I am usually a bit more composed than this."

Father Hickey pulled open the door to her car. As the raging wind tried to shut it, he stood aside to let her climb in. "Annie, what happened to you was just a dream, I am pretty sure. But I do know that the Lord will look out for your Mark, the same as he looks out for all of us."

Leaning into the car, he continued. "Annie, anything, anytime, I will be here, or just call, and I will come see you." Smiling, the young priest stood back up as the women started the car.

"Thank you, Father Hickey. I will remember that."

Shutting the door, the priest stood back. As Annie drove off, he strode back to the warmth of the church.

Hanging his vestments back in the closet, Father Hickey couldn't help but smile as he felt a wave of relief come over him. His first mass on his own. He had gotten rid of his vanity and shame all at once with his sermon. He had helped a woman deal a bit with the death of her husband. *All in all, a great start to a very cold day*, he thought. Turning, he looked down the aisle of pews and thought, *Wow, just an hour ago, these pews were*

*full, and people were listening to me speak the Word of our Lord God. Guess
I don't need one of them big parishes to do the work of the Lord.*

He knelt at the altar and said a short prayer of thanks.

Thank You, God.
For all You have given,
For all You have withheld,
For all You have withdrawn,
For all You have permitted,
For all You have prevented,
For all You have forgiven me,
For all You have prepared for me,
For the death You have chosen for me,
For the place You are keeping for me in Heaven,
For having created me to love you for eternity,
Thank You, God. Amen

Standing up, he thought, *Man, I could sure use some more coffee right
about now.* He shut the closet door and headed for the kitchen and the
hot pot of java.

CHAPTER 9

Pouring a cup of coffee, Father Hickey looked out the window and watched the boats move slowly through Point Judith Harbor. *If I get time today, I would like to get down to the harbor for a bit and look around*, he thought. Turning away from the window, he headed to the office. As he was sitting down at his desk, the phone rang. "Hello, Saint Peter's Church. Father Hickey speaking."

"Hi, Father," a man replied. "This is Ted Roberts. We talked yesterday. I was visiting my mother's grave. Do you remember me?"

"Yes, of course. How are you today, Mr. Roberts?"

"Fine, thank you, Father." After a moment of silence, Mr. Roberts asked, "Can I come by and talk with you today, Father Hickey?"

"Of course, of course. You and all are welcome here anytime. And if I can be of any help at all, please do not hesitate to ask for my spiritual guidance in any matter that you wish to talk with me about."

"Thanks, Father. I will drop by later today if that is good for you."

"Fine, Mr. Roberts. I will be here. Look forward to seeing you later today," Father Hickey said, and he heard the phone on the other end hang up.

"Well, I guess my day calendar is already starting to fill up with a few things to do. Guess it is time to get dressed," he said to his new friend, who was sitting on the windowsill, sunning herself in the morning sun. "Hmm, what shall I call you?" he said to the old orange cat as he scratched her behind her ear. A purring sound rose from the cat. "I think I shall call you Elsa because you look like a fat, lovable cow cat," he said with a laugh as the cat continue to purr.

Looking out the window over the graveyard, Father Hickey thought it was a busy day for mourners again. The little girl was again talking to the grave of her dog, Jackie. The big bear-man, Mike McDonough, was standing at the new grave that had no marker on it yet. *He seems to be talking to it, though most folks do talk to dead loved ones while at the grave. It gives them some sort of pathway to realize their grief.* That was according to the teacher Father Hickey had had back in the seminary school. Personally, Father Hickey thought it was a way to feel close to the loved one who had died. Slowly, though, with the passing of time, the closeness and loss would fade to a sad memory.

Over by the pile of brush and stone, the woman who had been there earlier had come back. She was also talking to what must be a grave, it seemed to the priest, though she did not seem sad, but very angry. After a moment, the woman turned and walked out of the graveyard.

Catching a glimpse of red hair passing by the window, Father Hickey looked down. Janie had come back to stand over the child's grave. She started to cry again. After laying a small white rose in front of the stone, she stood and quickly walked away, never once looking up at the window. *Well, this is very sad*, Father Hickey thought. "I wonder what is up with Janie and that child. Well, in time, maybe she will confide in me," he said to Elsa as he turned to the bedroom to get dressed for the long, busy day ahead.

"Hmm, what to wear today?" he said as he went through the clothes hanging in his closet. "Black seems to be in this year for the sharp-looking priest. Well, black, it will be," he said, laughing to himself as he pulled one of his three black shirts off a hanger. "And no priest should be without a set of matching black pants, shoes, and the white collar," he said to Elsa as she walked into the bedroom. After slowly climbing onto the bed, she curled up on the pillow and closed her eyes.

Reaching down to pat the cat, Father Hickey, laughing a bit, said. "Well, old lady, I guess that was quite a walk for you from the office to the bedroom." He sat on the edge of the bed and pulled his shoes on. "Well. Let's see if there is one more cup of coffee, and then maybe a quick trip to the harbor before Mr. Roberts comes in to talk," he said to the sleeping cart, and then he walked to the kitchen.

There was one full cup of the steaming brew left. Father Hickey started drinking coffee when he entered seminary school seven years ago. Some of the older students got him hooked on it to stay sharp during the tedious studying late into the night, followed by very strict 6:00 am prayer classes for two hours every day. Little sleep the night before became a common occurrence, and coffee soon became a prerequisite for long study hours at the seminary.

While walking back into the office, sipping the hot liquid, he was startled by a knock on the door to the living quarters. Opening the door, he was surprised to see Mr. Roberts all bundled up and stomping his feet to ward off the cold in his feet. "I know I am early, Father, but I really need to talk to you now, if I could," Mr. Roberts said with an almost desperate tone.

"Of course, of course. Please come in, Mr. Roberts. We can talk in my office," Father Hickey said, standing aside. "Can I get you something to drink, Mr. Roberts?"

"No thank you, Father. Please, the name is Ted, if that is ok with you, Father."

"Yes, Ted, that will be fine. Come in and have a seat," Father Hickey said as he opened the door to the office. "Sure, I can't get you something to drink, Ted?" Father Hickey asked again.

"No, Father, I am fine. Thanks for asking, though. Ted sat down and took a few moments to get his thoughts together. Shifting uncomfortably in his chair, he said, "Father, I know this sounds crazy, but my mother came and visited me last night." At this, Father Hickey leaned forward in his chair. "I know it sounds crazy," Ted said, panic in his voice, but she was there, just standing in my living room suddenly. The room got so cold I could see my breath in the air. 'Mother,' I said, 'what are you doing here? You are supposed to be dead.'" Ted was shaking now as if the cold he talked about had returned to surround him in the chair with its icy grasp. He started to weep.

Seeing that Ted was starting to panic, Father Hickey said in a quiet tone, "Ted. Ted, look at me. Are you sure that this was not some sort of a horrible nightmare you had last night?"

"No, Father, this was real. It was no nightmare. I was awake, and she was there in my living room."

"OK, then did she talk to you, Ted?"

"Yes, Father, she did speak to me," Ted said, shaking even more now in the chair. "She told me that the fisherman was hurting her, and I needed to make him stop. She was crying and crying. She knew what I had done to her. She told me I was going to pay for all the misery I had put her through in her life and that judgment time was close at hand for me. She said she was scared to go back to the graveyard because Abaddon was coming to take her away. She said death was not supposed to be like this and that Abaddon would visit the graveyard soon, very soon. Father, who is this Abaddon creature my mother spoke of?" Tears welled in Ted's eyes.

"Well, Ted," Father Hickey replied, trying to find the right words to describe this demon. In his heart, he knew there were no easy words for this one. "Abaddon has many names in many religions." Thinking back to his classes on demons, Father Hickey explained, "But in Christianity, Abaddon is chief demon of the seventh hierarchy. He is called the Destroyer. In the book of Revelation, Saint John called him the king of tormenting locusts. Many folks in religious circles call him Satan's right-hand man. But Ted, listen. This must be some sort of nightmare you had."

"No, Father, Ted shot back, panic rising in his voice. "This was as real as us talking right now.

"All right, Ted, let's just say you are right about all this." Father Hickey came around the desk and sat in a chair next to Ted. "Who is this fisherman your mother is talking about?"

Ted shook his head. "I do not know who or what the fisherman is, Father."

"Why would a mother threaten her child with such a demon?" Father Hickey asked. "There is nothing stronger than a mother's love for her child, Ted. Not to mention, I am not so sure Abaddon does personal favors for folks," he added with a smile, trying to calm Ted down.

"It was so real, Father Hickey," Ted said as he started to cry and shake from the cold that seemed to surround him once again. "It was so real, Father."

"Ted, why would your mother be so angry with you?"

"She thinks I took her home and put her in that damn nursing home and left her to die there." Ted stood and looked out the window over the graveyard. "She thinks I stole her savings and left her alone to die in that nursing home."

"Ted, listen to me. You just feel guilty that you couldn't do more," Father Hickey said, touching Ted on the shoulder. "You need to accept the fact that we always feel we could have done more. Even when, down deep, we know we couldn't have done more no matter what." Father Hickey grasped the shoulder harder. Walking back to his desk, he sat down and gave Ted a moment to think.

"Ted, come sit down for a bit, and let's continue our talk about this. I feel we can help you understand this better by talking some more about it and maybe set your mind at ease." Father Hickey pointed at the chair in front of the desk.

"No, Father. Thank you for your time, but I can tell you don't believe me. Hell, I barely believe this myself," Ted said in a quiet voice, almost a whisper, still looking out the window at his mother's grave. "I know she is not done with me. With all the bills and the cost of living, I just couldn't take care of her and me anymore. She was getting old and needed constant care. My mother got to the point where I had to feed her every day. I needed to work extra hours just to make ends meet. So, yes, I put her in the nursing home and sold that damn house." Ted clenched he fist as he continued to gaze at his mother's grave. "The state and the nursing home took every cent from the sale of the house. Just to make ends meet, I had to start painting closed cottages in the winter months. I had to move into that crap apartment over in Jerusalem when the house sold. I had nowhere to live."

Turning to look at the priest, Ted pleaded, "Father, what was I supposed to do? Doesn't she know that I had to live my life? I couldn't let us both go down. My mother could not help anymore, so I did the only thing I could. Right, Father Hickey? Right...?"

Ted, I believe what you have told me," Father Hickey in a soft tone. "The question is, what can you—what can we—do about it now? How can we help you come to grips with this?" The priest motioned to the chair again, trying to get Ted to sit down.

"There is nothing I can do now, Father. My mother is dead and beyond reach." Ted picked up his coat and walked to the door. "I am sorry to have bothered you with such foolishness. I am sure, after listening to the story, it is nothing more than a very bad nightmare I had, and I must deal with this myself."

"Ted, wait," Father Hickey said, getting up from his desk and following the other man out onto the porch. "Ted, listen to me. I am here to help in any way I can. Whether this was a dream or real doesn't matter right now." He stepped in front of Ted. "What matters is that you, that we, sit down so I can help you deal with all these feelings of remorse and abandonment that you just spoke to me about. Ted, I can tell you are not a bad man."

"Sorry to have bothered you, Father Hickey," Ted said as he stepped off the porch and headed towards his car, parked in front of the church. His boots crunched on the fresh snow.

"Ted, I am here anytime you need to talk," Father Hickey called out as Ted got into his car. "Damn," the priest said. "My second chance to help someone, and he is driving off in his car worse off than when he got here. Great job, Hickey." The screeching of a seagull behind him interrupted his rant.

As the priest turned to yell at the seagull, he caught a glimpse of a big man in fishing overalls, a black and red plaid jacket, and black wool pull-on cap. The man was standing by the cross, looking off towards the ocean, it seemed to the priest. Sitting on the marble bench in front of the cross was an old woman in a heavy blue wool jacket, praying with rosary beads. A Little boy played in the snow at her feet, making a tiny snowman with the fresh morning snow.

Opening the door, Father Hickey walked into the living quarters, and he shut the door behind him.

CHAPTER 10

---✠---

"Hey, Elsa girl," the priest said as he was greeted by the old cat at the door. "Want to go out for a bit?" But the cat just rubbed up against his leg. "Ok, maybe later. I saw some dry cat food and water in the kitchen this morning. Did you eat any of it today?" He picked up the cat and walked to the kitchen. "Well, old girl, I am not batting too well today. I hope the afternoon brings some luck for me." Putting the cat down in front of her food, Father Hickey poured another cup of coffee.

"Ahh, still hot. This is great," he said, showing the cat the cup. "Well, rumor has it this church has a car somewhere around here, and the keys are supposed to be in my desk drawer. Have you seen a church-mobile anywhere around here, Elsa?" he asked the cat as she continued to eat. "No, I take it, then, that I am off to find it, cat. Be back later."

He headed to the office to find the keys. Opening the top desk drawer, he found two sets: one was for an auto, and the other looked like a set of jailer keys. *Hmm, I have seen no jail cells in this church, so I will take the car keys and try to find the car,* he said to himself. Grabbing the keys and his jacket, he headed for the door.

Standing on the porch, Father Hickey shielded his eyes from the bright sunlight. "I need to get some sunglasses," he said, looking out over the graveyard. "Hmm, no more mourners. Guess the cold was a bit much today to stay too long." Walking down the stairs, he noticed they had been shoveled and salted again. "The giant man sure keeps up on this place." Trudging through the knee-high snow around the back of the church, Father Hickey found a garage with a shoveled driveway out to the street and a cleared walkway to the kitchen door. "Hmm, mental note to self," he said. "Use kitchen door to get to the garage."

He pulled up the garage door. "Great. No need for me to shovel now." The church-mobile was a new dark green Ford Expedition with all-wheel drive. "Well, this is nice," Father Hickey said, smiling as he thought back to the old Buick he'd gotten to drive at school. Bad seats, bad radio, and bad heat had all been included in that car. Opening the car door, Father Hickey climbed in and shut the door to keep the cold out. "Hope this beast heats quick." Fumbling to put the key in the ignition, he turned the key, and the engine quickly came to life. "Off we go," he said as he put the car into drive and slowly pulled out of the garage.

The road to Galilee was plowed, and the snow was starting to melt on the road from use. "Let's see if I can remember how to get to the seaport." He turned on the radio.

"Time for local news," came a voice. "Well, it seems the terror of two years ago has come back to Galilee. Local police report that upwards of fifty cats were killed in various places in Galilee and surrounding areas. You may recall that a few years ago, a similar problem happened over the course of a week in which dozens of cats were killed. A rabid dog was later blamed for the cat killings and was euthanized at the local pet shelter."

Wow, fifty cats. The giant man was not kidding, Father Hickey thought, turning the channel to find some music. "Well, at least this car has heat," he said as he felt the warmth of the heater, so much that he had to turn the heat down a notch.

As he slowed for a stop sign, he looked to his left. "Ahh, the fisherman memorial. I know where I am now." In front of the memorial, a small child played in the snow under the watchful eye of a man who appeared to be the one he had seen in the graveyard earlier today wearing the plaid jacket. Stopping for a moment, Father Hickey waited for a snowplow to go through the intersection. When he looked back at the memorial, the child and man were gone. "Just take a left here and straight into the port," the priest said above the blaring radio.

The masts of the fishing fleet came into view as the priest drove towards the port of Galilee. The streets were alive with activity as the fishing boats were unloading their weekly catches. *Looks like a very busy day here today*, the priest thought as he slowed the car to let some folks cross the street. Looking across the street, he could see the Crow's Nest, and it looked to be very busy. *The men on the boats haven't had a drink in a week and can't wait for the warmth of Mike's Irish whiskey, I bet*, thought Father Hickey with a smile.

Moving slowly forward again, he saw a sign that said, "Salty Brine State Beach," with an arrow pointing straight ahead. Driving a few more blocks through the center of town, Father Hickey came to the beach and a sign that said, "Parking."

The sound of the Atlantic Ocean crashing against the rocks and spraying the parking lot with sea spray greeted the priest as he climbed out of the car. The screams of seagulls filled the air. "Wow. You could never see this in Kansas." Pulling his coat tightly around his neck, the priest walked down a concrete ramp and towards the roar of the beach waves.

The beach was dotted with people. A man waving a metal detector back and forth over the sand walked by, nodding to the priest. A red ball rolled to the priest's feet and bounced off one. The ball was suddenly grabbed by a large black dog that ran away with it.

"Good boy, Snickers," a man said as the dog brought the ball to him and placed it in his hand. Walking over to Father Hickey, the man held out his hand. "Hello, my name is Abraham, and this good boy is Snickers." He knelt and hugged the dog. "And you, my friend, are Father Hickey," he said to the priest.

"Yes, I am. How did you know that?" Father Hickey asked.

Laughing, the man said, "I was at mass this morning. And I must tell you I was very impressed with the sermon, Father Hickey."

"Why, thank you, Abraham. I must tell you I was very nervous about the whole thing. I was hoping that when I got here, Father Gilday would help me get through my first few masses." Father Hickey reached down to pet the dog.

"Yes, Father Gilday was quite a priest and a good friend." Abraham threw the ball again. "Get it, Snickers."

"Did you know him well?" Father Hickey asked.

"For the better part of the fifty-plus years, he was assigned here. Father Gilday, now, that man had a special way about him. Never too busy to listen to the problems of folks around here. And he wasn't a bad chess player." Abraham took the ball from the dog and threw it once again down the beach. "Go get it, boy!" he yelled.

"Come, let's walk, Father Hickey. These old bones must keep moving, or they will freeze solid in this weather." Abraham slipped his arm into the young priest's. "When Father Gilday first got here, like you, he was mad because he had worked and studied so hard in seminary school. Father Gilday thought he should have been assign to one of the more prestigious churches in the country. He was so bitter when he got here. He told me once that he almost left the priesthood because he did not feel his worth.

"Years later, Father Gilday was given the opportunity to go to a big parish in New York City. He turned the offer flat down because he said it was clear that this is where God had deemed, he be. It was here that he could and did the best for the most folks. You, my young friend, have been chosen to replace a great man and a good friend." Abraham let go of Father Hickey's arm. "I am sure you will not disappoint the memory of Father Gilday. But more importantly, you will find yourself in all this. God knows what he is doing, and you have been sent here for a reason, Father Hickey. Ahh, I see my ride has come for me."

Abraham called Snickers over. "Well, it is time to go home and rest these cold, weary bones... It was good to meet you, Father Hickey. I will see you tomorrow at mass." He held out his hand.

"Same, Abraham. It was so nice to meet you and Snickers."

They shook, and then Abraham and Snickers walked slowly up the ramp to a waiting car. *I should get me a dog*, Father Hickey thought as he picked up the ball Snickers had left behind on the wet beach.

While walking back up the beach ramp to his car, Father Hickey could not help but think what Abraham had meant when he'd said God had sent him here for a reason. *Seems he has firsthand knowledge of what destiny has planned for him*, Father Hickey thought. *He knew Father Gilday for fifty years. That is true friendship.* Reaching the top of the ramp, he looked back at the beach and saw dark, ominous clouds rolling in off the horizon, towards the beach. The ferry horn sounded as the boat left the harbor and headed towards Block Island.

Looking out as the ferry passed, Father Hickey could make out a few brave souls standing outside on the deck in the stinging, salty wind, and waves as they crashed over the bow of the ferry. "Sometime soon, I am going to take the ride to Block Island," Father Hickey said as the ferry sounded its horn again. "But I will wait until it is much warmer out." Climbing into his car, he started the motor and drove back towards the Crow's Nest.

Pulling his car into a parking spot there, Father Hickey climbed out and started for the front door. "Father Hickey?" A woman called out as she crossed the street towards the young priest. She was all bundle up, with a scarf wrapped around her face so all he could see was her eyes inside the hooded parks she was wearing to ward off the cold. "Father Hickey, it is a pleasure to finally meet you," the woman said as she reached out and took his hand in hers. "I loved your sermon this morning. It was so moving to listen to. Father Gilday would have been very proud of you today."

"Thank you. And you are?" Father Hickey said as he tried to retrieve his hand from the grasp of the woman.

"Oh, forgive me." She let go of his hand. "My name is Mary," she said as she pulled back the hood of her parka. "Ahh, that is better," she said, pulling down the scarf. "I am so glad to see you again, Father."

"And it is nice to see you again, Mary," Father Hickey said, laughing as he realized that he had met Mary just a few hours ago after service. "That is quite an outfit you are wearing."

"Yes, it does seem a bit much, but it is better to overdress than underdress in the winter months in New England," Mary said as she tried to fix her hair. "You could use a pair of boots yourself, Father Hickey." She looked down at the priest's wet-sneaker-clad feet.

"Yes, I think I will be picking up a pair or two this week," the father replied as he stamped his feet on the wooden sidewalk to knock off the snow and slush.

"Are you going into the Crow's Nest, Father?" Mary asked, nodding towards the bar door.

"Yes, I was planning to. Is there some reason why I should not?" Father Hickey asked with a nod and a grin towards the door.

"Hell, no," Mary said, laughing. "Just be careful of Mike's Irish whiskey. Many a morning, I wished I had taken that advice the night before. Well, nice to meet you, Father Hickey. See you at service tomorrow." Mary pulled up her hood, turned, and headed back across the street.

Quite a woman, Father Hickey thought as she disappeared into the slow-moving crowd. *I guess I had better get me some boots soon.* He looked down at his wet black sneakers. *Gloves would be a good idea, too.*

Opening the door to the Crow's Nest, he was assaulted by the smell of smoke and beer.

CHAPTER 11

⟡

"Tommy, over here," came a call from the far corner of the bar. "Tommy, over here," came the call again, above the noise in the bar.

Looking in the direction of the voice, Father Hickey could see the giant man, Mike, waving him over to a table he was sitting at with two other men. Making his way through the crowd, the priest reached the table and accepted the seat the bear-man pointed at.

"Have a seat, Tommy, have a seat. Good to see you," the bear-man said. "I was getting a little worried you would not be joining us for lunch today. Tommy, I want you to meet two dear friends of mine. This gentleman to my right is Samuel, and this other bloke over there is Jonah. I have known these men all my life, pretty much."

"And a damn shame for us," Samuel said, laughing. "Hello, Father Hickey." he reached across the table to shake the priest's hand. "Heard your sermon this morning at mass, and I have to say it was very special to all of us who were there today."

"Same for me," said Jonah as he reached across the table to shake the priest's hand.

"Mike tells us this is your first assignment, Tommy," Samuel said, and then he took a drink from the beer mug in front of him.

"Yes, it is," Father Hickey replied above the noise of the bar.

"So, how do you like our little seaport of Galilee so far?" Jonah asked.

"Well, it has been a bit cold, to say the least. Mary told me I need to get a few pairs of boots to get through the winter here."

"Ahh, Mary, she is quite a gal," the bear-man said, "always looking to make sure a man is taken care of. That is the true mother in her."

"Hello, Father." Janie came into view with a beer and a menu for the priest.

"Janie, good to see you," Father Hickey said above the noise.

"Here ya go, Father. When you are ready to order, just give it to Mike." Without another word, she left.

"Well, she seems a bit busy today," Father Hickey said, looking over at the bear-man, Mike.

"Not really, Tommy. She just has a few things on her mind right now. And now that Father Gilday is gone, she is at a bit of a loss for spiritual guidance." Mike took another drink of his beer.

"No offense, Father Hickey. She does not know you yet," Samuel added from across the table.

"Yes, she and Father Gilday were best of friends for going on six or seven years now," said Jonah.

"'Friends' is putting it mildly," Mike added. "They were more like dad and daughter, always doing things together. Father Gilday once told me she was a very troubled woman, but he would not go say anything else about it. Well, Tommy, what would you like to eat? It's on Jonah today." He laughed.

"Well, Mike, everything looks good, so I guess I will just go with the fish and chips."

"Great, Tommy, and a cup of chowda to start it off is how we do it around here," the bear said as he called Janie over and gave her the priest's order.

Lunch and the small talk flew by, and when Father Hickey looked at his watch, it was now 5:30, and the afternoon sun was beginning to set outside. It had started to lightly snow an hour ago, and now it was falling at a rapid clip, covering the streets outside. "Well, gentlemen, I must be going," he said to the men at the table. "I am still not sure what I am supposed to do daily, but I am pretty sure it must be more than this, not that I mind this." He laughed. "Jonah, thanks for lunch. Samuel, it has been a pleasure meeting you."

"Same here, Father Hickey," Samuel said, standing to shake the priest's outstretched hand.

"Mike, in my short time here, you have made me feel very welcome in Galilee, and I want to thank you for that."

"Ahh, no problem at all, Tommy," Mike said as he slapped the priest on the back. "Do not forget to thank Janie on your way out. The cook likes to know her cooking is appreciated."

"Sure, I was going to stop by the kitchen and say good-bye anyways," Father Hickey said, and he turned and walked towards the barroom kitchen.

"Hey, Janie, got a minute?" Father Hickey said as he stood at the kitchen door.

"Sure, Father, what can I do for you?"

"Well, nothing, Janie. Is there anything I can do for you?" the priest asked in a quiet tone.

"No, Father, I am fine."

"I understand that you and Father Gilday became very good friends over the years. I know we have not known each other very long, but if you give me a chance, I bet we could become good friends, too. But either way, I just wanted to tell you the food was great, and I really enjoyed the fish and chips. I gotta tell you that was the first time I ever had clam chowder, or as Mike says—"

Janie chipped in, "Chowda."

"Yes," Father Hickey said, laughing a bit. "Chowda. Janie, I mean it. Anytime you feel the need to talk about anything or nothing," Father Hickey said as he started to turn and leave the bar.

"Father, wait up," Janie called. She came up to him and handed him a paper bag. "I made you a few corned beef sandwiches. I know it is silly, but Father Gilday loved them, and I thought you might, too."

"Janie, I love corned beef sandwiches. I think it is a priest thing." Father Hickey took the bag. "Remember, anytime."

"Thanks, Father," Janie said, and she turned and walked back to the kitchen.

Well, let's see how I drive in the snow, Father Hickey said to himself as he headed out the door and into the cold of the late afternoon.

"So, Michael, do you think he will be up to the task?" Samuel asked as he watched the young priest walk out the door.

"Well, time will tell. It always does. But yes, I think he is up to the task," Mike said, and he took another drink from his beer bottle.

Watching the priest walk by the window, Jonah chipped in, "Yes, let's pray this young priest is up to such a task."

As he drove slowly out of town, Father Hickey had a hard time seeing the road due to the swirling snow. On the radio, a severe weather alert was being broadcasted for most of the New England area. "Great, more snow," he said, turning the radio station to a music channel. While slowing for the stop sign near the fishing memorial, Father Hickey looked over to see a large man with a plaid jacket, knitted pull-down cap, and rubber overalls, the kind a fisherman uses to work on the boats, standing in front of the memorial, smoking a cigarette as he looked at the priest.

Looks like the man I saw in the graveyard this morning, the priest thought. Looking to make sure no other car was coming, Father Hickey looked at the memorial again, only to see the man had vanished. *Man, he is quick. Must have gone inside.* He started to drive once again.

When he pulled the car into the snow-filled driveway, he pushed the door opener above the visor. Pulling into the garage, he hoped he would not have to walk all the way around the church to get in like last night.

It is way too cold for that, he thought. Grabbing the bag of sandwiches Janie had made, he climbed out of the car and headed for the kitchen door. While climbing the stairs, the priest stopped for a moment. "Well, here goes," he said. Pushing the door open, he stepped into the warmth of the kitchen. Yes, it was open. *Point for the home team*, he thought as he shut the door behind him.

"Well, hey, Elsa girl," the priest said as the old orange cat came slowly walking into the kitchen. "So, did you worry about me while I was gone?" He bent down and picked up the purring cat. "Hey, old lady, that is quite a motor you have there. I have some corned beef sandwiches. Want to try some with me in a bit?" He put the cat down in front of the water bowl. Taking off his jacket, he switched on the television, grabbed a beer from the refrigerator, and headed to his office.

Switching on the computer, he looked out the window towards the graveyard as the computer booted up. The snowstorm was now in full force as evening came upon Galilee. Catching a glimpse of movement in the graveyard, Father Hickey looked down just in time to see a small black and white dog run out of the graveyard and disappear in the swirling snow. "Well, there you are," the priest said to the disappearing dog. "I hope you have a warm place to go tonight. As they say, 'not a night fit for man or beast.'" He took a drink of the beer in his hand.

"You have mail," a computer voice said behind him. "Ahh, all booted up and ready to go," he said, sitting down at the computer terminal. Clicking on the mailbox, Father Hickey could see three emails were junk, one was from his brother, and one was for Father Gilday. Opening the email from his brother, Father Hickey started to laugh. It was pictures of their older brother in a very funny cowboy hat. Under the pictures were the words "Horse Cartwright." Laughing, the priest got up and headed for the kitchen and the corned beef sandwiches.

Sitting down at the table, he flipped through channels on the television as he opened the bag of sandwiches Janie had given him.

"The storm approaching off the Atlantic promises to dump a foot to more than eighteen inches of snow over the next eight hours, depending on a cold front coming down from Canada," the local news reporter said from outside somewhere in this cold weather as the wind whipped the snow all around him.

Laughing to himself, the priest said, "What will they do next for ratings?" as he pulled off a piece of the corned beef and, as promised, shared it with Elsa. "Here you go, girl. Not sure if a cat should eat corned beef, but you do seem to like it," he told her as he stroked her head.

Turning the channel again, Father Hickey came across a hockey game: the Boston Bruins against the New York Islanders. He thought back to his high school days when he'd played for the junior varsity hockey team back in his senior year in high school. He was never quite aggressive enough for the varsity squad, the coach had told him, but he was a good junior varsity player and should be happy just being on the squad. "Hmm, boy, was he right," the priest said to Elsa. "Here ya go, girl." He gave her another piece of corned beef. Looking out the window over the television, Father Hickey could only see his reflection; it was snowing so much now that the snow blocked out any view of the outside. "Well, let's make sure we are locked up for the evening, Elsa, and then maybe a little reading and then bed. Sound good, old girl?" The priest stood up from the table, grabbed his beer, and walked out of the kitchen.

In the living room, Father Hickey noticed a large piece of yellow paper hanging on the wall next to the door leading into the church. Pulling the note off the wall, the priest began to read: "Father Hickey, if you do not mind, please make sure church is locked up every night. When I got here this morning to shovel, the front door to the church had been left unlocked. We have had problems with several break-ins over the last few years, so we lock the church after 7:00 p.m. Thanks, Jedrek Szymanowska."

Laughing a bit to himself, Father Hickey said, "Yes, I can do this." Setting his beer on a table next to the door, the priest walked into the church.

The lights were all on. The candles at the altar burned brightly, flickering in the drafty air of the church. Walking between the pews, Father Hickey reached the church front doors, and he locked them. "There we go, Mr. Szymanowska. Per your request, the church doors are now locked."

He tried to look out the window, but the snow had covered it in an icy crust. *This is going to be one cold night*, the priest thought as he headed back down the pews. Kneeling at the altar, he began his evening prayer.

"Dear Father, I feel so content as I get ready for bed. And I believe this wonderful feeling is because of the good fortune that came my way today. Thank You for helping to make this a successful day in my life. It has given me hope that even better things are in store for me. I truly appreciate the many gifts I receive from You. May I always be worthy of them. Please continue to stay by my side, leading me to even greater joy and success, and after this peaceful night of sleep, may tomorrow be another fine day in Your care. Thank You so much... Goodnight, dear Lord."

Making the sign of the cross, Father Hickey stood, took one more look down the pew aisle, and said to the church, "Well, it appears I have successfully locked the church this cold night." He made the sign of the cross in the air and walked out of the church, shutting the door behind him.

As he watched the young priest walk through the door, the old man in black, sitting in the front pew, gave a small smile, nodded, and turned back to his prayers.

CHAPTER 12

"Well, Elsa, time for a bit of reading and then bed," the priest said as he shut off the television in the kitchen. Picking up the cat, he headed for the office to read and plan his sermon for the next day. "Here you go, old girl," he said as he gently put the cat on the couch in the office. "Hmm, let us see what Father Gilday had to read here," he said to the cat as he started to look at the many books on the shelves. *Wow, Father Gilday had quite a collection of books here*, the priest thought as his eyes came to rest on *The Fundamentals of Catholic Dogma*, by Ludwig Ott.

I know this book. He thought back to a paper he had written on this very principle his second year at the seminary. It had caused quite a stir and long hours of debate in class and earned him a perfect grade that year in Concept and Object of Theology class. Putting the book back, Father Hickey smiled as he pulled the next book off the shelf. "Perhaps the best book of all time," he said to Elsa, and he sat on the couch, opened the book, and began to read.

"In my younger and more vulnerable years, my father gave me some advice that I have been turning over in my head ever since. 'Whenever you feel like criticizing anyone,' he told me, 'just remember that not all the people in this world have had all the advantages you have had.' Ahh, *The Great Gatsby*," the priest said as he stroked the purring cat. "No one could write like Fitzgerald."

As he read, the barking of a dog outside could be heard echoing in the wind. Elsa began to growl. "Do not worry, old girl," he said to the cat as he stroked her head. "We are not going out tonight, and that dog is not coming in."

Father Hickey read for a few hours until he could barely keep his eyes open any longer. "Come on, old girl," the priest said, looking down at the cat. "Time for bed." He picked up the cat and headed for the bedroom.

Laying Elsa on the bed, Father Hickey changed into his sweatpants and Kansas Jayhawks shirt. Kneeling at his bed, the priest began his evening prayer.

Lord, make me an instrument of your peace.
Where there is hatred, let me sow love.
Where there is injury, pardon.
Where there is doubt, faith.
Where there is despair, hope.
Where there is darkness, light.
Where there is sadness, joy.
O Divine Master, grant that I may not so much.
Seek to be consoled as to console,
Not so much to be understood as to understand,
Not so much to be loved as to love,
For it is in giving that we receive.
It is in pardoning that we are pardoned.
It is in dying that we awake to eternal life.
Amen

Climbing into his bed and shutting off the table lamp, Father Hickey quickly fell into a deep sleep. The faint sound of a cat screaming in its last moment of life from outside the church had Elsa the cat growling in a low tone at the window from the safety of the bed as she moved closer to the sleeping priest for protection.

The radio alarm clicked on, and the 68 RKO Boston morning show started. "Good morning, New England. It is 7:00 am. If you do not have to work today, then just stay home. Over a foot of snow was dumped from Connecticut to New Hampshire over the evening hours, and the driving conditions are treacherous out there today. Local and state officials are asking all non-essential personnel to stay home today and let the D.P.W. crews get out there and do the work of clearing the roads."

Rolling over, Father Hickey looked at the clock. "Morning already? Damn," he said as he started to rise from his bed. Stretching on the bed, Elsa yawned as he rubbed her belly. "Good morning, old girl. And how did you sleep last night?" he asked as he put on his slippers. Then he headed for the kitchen to start some coffee for his morning caffeine fix.

"Good morning, Father Hickey," Mrs. Szymanowska said as he entered the kitchen.

"Oh, Mrs. Szymanowska. I am sorry. I forgot you would be here today," the father said as he realized what he was wearing.

"Please, Father, just call me Maria, and not to worry. I have sons your age, and they still cannot dress correctly, either" she said, handing the embarrassed priest a cup of steaming-hot coffee.

"Thank you, Maria," he said, sitting at the table. The sound of a snowblower could be heard from outside. The local morning news was on the television.

"Our top stories today are, of course, the weather, but we are also following the story of a double rape and homicide of two women during the night in Tuckertown, Rhode Island. More after these messages from our sponsors," the announcer said.

"What a shame," Maria said, turning away from the television and back to the breakfast she was making.

"Shame?" the priest asked, sipping his coffee as he looked out the window to watch the snow fall.

"Yes, those poor girls raped and murdered last night just down the road in Tuckertown," she said, almost in a panic.

"Ahh, good morning, Father Hickey," the giant man said as he entered the kitchen from outside. The cold wind blew in some snow as he shut the door.

"Good morning, Jedrek." Looks like we got a bit of snow last night," the priest replied.

"Yes, I suppose you could say that" Jedrek said as he hung his jacket by the door and sat at the table with the priest.

Setting a cup of coffee in front of her husband, Mrs. Szymanowska continued with her story. "As I was saying to Father Hickey, what a shame about the two women over in Tuckertown."

"Yes, it has been a long time since something like this happened around these parts," the giant man said as he drank his coffee.

"The news reporter says it seems like a copycat killing, like the fisherman killer we had here about five years ago," Mrs. Szymanowska said as she refilled the priest's cup of coffee.

"Fisherman killer?" the priest asked as he drank some more of the hot java.

"Yes, a few years ago, we had several rapes and killings here in the Galilee area," said the giant man. "It turned out it was a local fisherman who would ship out for some of the longer hauls, so it was hard to find him. Anyways, he was caught in the act by a few of the locals and was killed while trying to escape them. It was not pretty, what they did to him. Some say he was stuck full of fishing hooks, wrapped up in a dragger net, and thrown into the Atlantic to drown. His body washed up on Point Judith a few days later."

"How did they know he was the one?" Father Hickey asked as he leaned forward.

"Well, it seems that his last rape victim did not die. One night, she spotted him coming out of the Crow's Nest, and well, that is when the locals took it into their own hands." The giant held his cup up for more java.

"Father Hickey, you don't know?" Mrs. Szymanowska chipped in as she placed a plate of bacon and scrambled eggs in front of the priest. "The fisherman is buried in the graveyard right outside the church."

A knock on the kitchen door interrupted the conversation. In walked Mike McDonough. "Good morning, all," he said. "A rough day out for man or beast. I haven't seen this much snow since, hmm, last week," the bear-man said with a laugh.

"Good morning, Michael," Mrs. Szymanowska said, putting a cup of hot coffee in front of the bear.

"Ahh, thank you, Maria. This is just what my old bones need on a cold morning such as this." He lifted the hot brew to his lips.

"Mike, what do you think about the murders last night over in Tuckertown?" the giant asked.

"Yes, I heard what happened. If I didn't know better, I'd say the fisherman is back in town."

"But that cannot be, because he is buried outside," Mrs. Szymanowska said, cutting into the conversation.

"True enough. Buried right next to Father Gilday."

"Wait, so you are telling me someone who committed the greatest of all sins, murder, is buried in a Catholic graveyard and, to top it all off, buried next to the last priest of this parish?" Father Hickey asked with amazement.

"Well, Tommy, it is not really a Catholic graveyard," the bear-man said. "It was just part of the poorhouse that used to be here, a pauper gravesite next to the church. So, it was just adopted by the church when the poorhouses were torn down. As far as Father Gilday, he wanted to be buried there. Always said this church was his home now and this is where he was to rest so he could watch over things here."

"This is all news to me," Father Hickey said, shaking his head.

"Yes, the two women were found dead early this morning, badly beaten and raped. It is also my understanding that these women were living in the same home as the last intended victim of the fisherman. You know, the one who spotted him here in Galilee." The bear-man drank some more of the hot java.

"Have the police found the person who did this?" Father Hickey asked.

"No, not a clue, is what I heard this morning on the news, Tommy," the bear replied, holding out his cup, which was now empty.

"It is my understanding that some of the locals took justice into their own hands when this man became known to them," Father Hickey said, looking at the bear-man.

"Yes, it is true. Justice was a bit swift in this matter."

"And nothing was done to the folks who did this?"

"No, Tommy, it was handled here by the folks it most affected and left at that. Oh, questions were asked. The Rhode Island State Police came into town and questioned everyone in town and on the boats. Nobody the police talked to knew anything about what happened. Not even Father Gilday would talk. He forgave every person who had a hand in it, through confession." The bear-man looked out the window as the falling snow continued with no sign of letting up anytime soon.

"I need to get on with the shoveling and cleaning the cat blood off the walkway," Mr. Szymanowska said in his thick Polish accent.

"More dead cats, Jedrek?" Father Hickey asked, looking at the giant man.

"Yes. Near as I can count, around ten last night. Must be a pack of wild dogs, though they are not dragging them away to eat, which is strange. Mass in one hour, Father Hickey." Jedrek put on his wool parka and headed out the door, closing it behind him.

"Tommy, I came over to ask a favor of you," the bear-man said as he leaned towards the priest.

"Of course, Mike. What can I do for you?" the priest asked as he lifted his cup of java for a drink.

"I need you to talk with Jamie. She is having a very hard time without Father Gilday here to guide her through these times."

"I offered her my shoulder yesterday, Mike, but she said everything was fine," the priest said, putting down his cup.

"Yes, I know," Mike said. "She told me and asked me what I thought about it. I told her you, my friend, are a man of God and close to her age, so maybe you would be able to connect quicker with her and her problem."

"Do you know what is bothering her, Mike?"

"Yes, Tommy, I do know what it is. But that is something she must tell you. I have kept her friendship all these years by keeping her problems between us. I do know she is now willing to talk with you the next chance she gets. So, all I am asking you, Tommy, is that you just listen and try not to judge her in this matter." The bear-man held out his hand and rose to leave.

"Sure, Mike, I will keep an open mind because God loves us all and we all are granted forgiveness from Him."

"Thanks, Tommy. And thanks for the coffee, Maria. See you at mass."

As the bear-man left, Maria replied, "Bye, Michael. See you soon," and then she also left the kitchen, saying she had laundry to do before church.

Picking up his coffee, Father Hickey started for his bedroom to get dressed for what he was sure would be a long day. Elsa was just waking up on the bed when he entered the room. "Hey, old girl," he said as he reached down and scratched the cat's belly. "So, it looks like you had a good night's sleep."

Looking out the window, the priest could see that for the time being, it had stopped snowing. Looking towards Point Judith, the priest saw the fishing fleet leaving for a day of fishing. "Man, you gotta give it to the fishermen here, Elsa. They are truly a rare breed of person. Heading out in all weather."

Sipping his coffee, Father Hickey opened the closet door and began to dress for a cold day.

CHAPTER 13

"Well, Elsa, black does seem to be my style," the priest said to the cat. Looking in the mirror, Father Hickey thought, *Things never change. I can get dressed in my sleep.*

He grabbed his coffee cup and headed for the kitchen to refill it. As he was pouring another cup, he heard the church door open. Walking into the living room, the priest was greeted by Rickey, the altar boy. "Good morning, Father," Rickey said, a smile covering his face.

"And good morning to you, Rickey. Would you like some coffee?" Father Hickey said with a smile.

"No, Father, I am not old enough for coffee."

"Oh, well, ok, if you are sure about that," Father Hickey said with a disappointed frown and then a smile. "So, what can I do for you today, Rickey?"

"Nothing, Father. We have the church all set up, and Mr. Szymanowska is just about done with the shoveling."

"Great," the priest replied. "I will see you in a bit, then. I need to go to my office and do a few things first, Rickey."

"Sure, Father, we will see you soon. We have everything under control for you in the church." With a smile, Rickey turned and headed back towards the church.

What a nice young man, Father Hickey thought as he headed towards his office.

Sitting down at his desk, the priest began to write a few notes for the service. A knocking on the window interrupted his thoughts. Outside stood the little girl he had seen there the last two days, waving at him. When he waved back, she gave him a shy little grin.

Turning back to his work, the little girl knocked on the window again and motioned for the priest to come outside. Laughing a bit, the priest pointed at himself and then made little finger movements like walking outside. Laughing, the little girl nodded. "Oh, you want me," the priest said, pointing at his chest once more and making the finger-walking movement. The little girl laughed and nodded again. Grabbing his jacket from the hook near the door, Father Hickey headed outside to meet the little girl.

Upon opening the door, Father Hickey was almost blown back into the living quarters by the Atlantic wind as it came off the ocean like a fast-moving freight train. Catching his balance, the priest grabbed the railing and started down the stairs. At the gate, he was met by the little girl and her mother.

"Father, I am so sorry Emma was banging on your window and bothering you like that."

"Oh, please, it was no bother at all. I am here to be bothered," the priest said with a laugh. So, Emma, my name is Father Hickey." He knelt so he was face to face with the little girl. "I can hardly see you in there, Emma." He opened her hood just a bit. "Ahh, there you are," he said to the smiling girl. "Now, what is it that you would like to talk to me about?"

"My dog is bad, Father. My dog is very bad," the little girl said, making a mean face.

"Bad? Why is that?" the priest asked, looking up at Emma's mother.

"Oh, Father, Emma's dog, Jackie, has been dead for almost a year now. We buried her in the graveyard last spring with Father Gilday."

"But Mommy, tell him about the cats that are dead," Emma said, pulling on her mother's jacket.

"Yes, Emma, I will. Anyway, her dog, Jackie, killed a bunch of cats, so we had to put her to sleep. Emma was hysterical about it. Father Gilday told her that he would make sure God would watch over Jackie, so we buried Jackie here, and Father Gilday blessed the grave and promised Emma Jackie would go to Heaven and be with other dogs and wait for Emma to come someday so they could play again. That dog loved this little girl so much."

Emma began crying for her dog.

"Emma, there is no need to cry. Now, why do you think Jackie would leave Heaven, come here, and chase cats?" Father Hickey said in a calm voice as he wiped away a tear from her red cheeks.

"Because I was playing with her last night and she had blood on her feet and mouth," Emma said, and she began to cry again.

Looking at the mother, Father Hickey asked. "Did you see Jackie last night?"

"No. I did hear Emma talking to Jackie last night in her room, but she has a stuffed dog she calls Jackie, so I did not pay much mind to it until…" The mother stopped mid-sentence like she had just realized something.

"Until what?" the priest asked as he stood to face Emma's mother.

"Well, I thought I heard a dog barking in her room, and then she screamed, 'Stop hurting me.' So, I ran into her room but found her alone. She told me Jackie was being bad and was pulling her shirt and would not let go."

"Emma, I am sure you just had a bad dream," Father Hickey said. He looked down at the little girl as she clutched her mother's leg. "Emma, Jackie is in Heaven with all the other dogs."

"You don't believe me," Emma said, starting to cry again.

"Yes, I do, Emma. Dreams can make everything very real." Father Hickey knelt to face Emma. Wiping away her tears, he said, "But if it will make you feel better, let's go talk to Jackie right now."

"Now?" Emma asked.

"Yeah, now. Come on." Father Hickey took the girl's hand, and they walked towards the pet's grave.

"Hi, Jackie. My name is Father Hickey. I am here with Emma and her mother to talk with you today." The priest knelt in the soft snow next to the grave. "My friend Emma says that you have been visiting her the last few nights. That is ok." The priest smiled at the little girl. "But she needs her sleep, so if you could be a little quieter and not bite her clothes, it would be a big help to her." Making the sign of the cross, Father Hickey stood up.

"Emma, if Jackie starts any more trouble, please give me a call, and we will talk with her again." The priest patted the child on the head.

"It's getting a bit cold out, Emma. We need to go," the child's mother said as she held out her hand. "Thank you, Father Hickey. I hope this works. Emma has quite the imagination." The mother turned to walk away.

"Bye, Jackie," Emma called as they walked towards a car parked on the street.

Well, Father Hickey thought, *this is getting a bit weird. First, a dead mother bothering her son. Now a playful dead dog.*

He headed for the church to get ready for the morning service. As he climbed the three steps to the living quarters, he was met at the door by Rickey, dressed in his altar boy clothes. Little Glenn stood behind him.

"Father, we are all ready," Rickey said as he tried to keep the door between him and the cold wind that tried to get in.

"Thanks, Ricky. Give me just a moment to get ready. I will be right there," Father Hickey said as he shut the outside door. Brushing past Ricky and Glenn, he headed for his bedroom to change.

Shaking his head, Ricky headed back to the church, followed by Glenn.

The mass went smoothly, Father Hickey thought as he said good-bye to the last of the guests and shut the church door. Glenn and Ricky were busy putting away the Bibles and cleaning the pews. Mrs. Szymanowska had gone back to the living quarters to tidy up before she and the giant man, Mr. Szymanowska, headed for home. The giant man had gone back outside to finish plowing. Kneeling before the altar, Father Hickey thanked God.

Almighty God, my Eternal Father,
From the fullness of my soul, I adore You.
I am deeply grateful that You have made me
In Your image and likeness,
And that You ever hold me in Your loving embrace.
Direct me to love You with all my heart, with all my soul.
Thank You, God, for sending me here to this place to do your bidding.
Amen.

Making the sign of the cross, Father Hickey stood and smiled at Glenn as he came towards him. "Good job today, Glenn," he said as he touched the boy on the head.

"Thanks, Father," Glenn replied with a shy smile. "Ricky says we are all done, Father Hickey, and we will see you tomorrow if everything is ok with you."

"I am very fortunate to have two men such as you and your brother to help me with my first parish. Thank you, Glenn, for helping me out these first couple of days."

"Glenn, Dad is here," Ricky called out as he peered out the church window.

"Well, gotta go, Father. Bye," Glenn said, and he ran to the door his brother was holding open for him.

"Thanks, Ricky," Father Hickey called out to the waving boy as he shut the church door behind them. *Nice kids*, the priest thought, and he headed for the warmth of the living quarters.

"Father Hickey, you have a visitor in your office," Mrs. Szymanowska said as she handed him a cup of hot coffee.

"Visitor? Who is it?" Father Hickey asked as he took the coffee.

"Mr. Roberts said he had to talk to you. Been in your office since mass started." Mrs. Szymanowska started back towards the kitchen, but then she stopped. "Oh, Father, we are just about done, so we will see you in a few days if that is ok with you."

"Yes, of course," the priest replied. "Oh, Mrs. Szymanowska, how am I doing so far?" he asked with a smile.

"Funny you would ask that, Father. Last night, my husband and I were talking about that very thing." She smiled back and then went into the kitchen.

I should have known better, the priest thought with a smile as he headed for his office and Mr. Roberts.

CHAPTER 14

Opening the door to his office, Father Hickey walked in to see Ted Roberts standing at the window looking out into the graveyard. "Father Gilday told me she would be at peace here," Ted said without turning around to look at the priest. "He told me she was with God and would be at peace. Father Gilday told me I did everything I could. I was not at fault." Turning to look at the priest, he continued. "Father, I have done nothing to deserve this anguish my mother is putting me through. I did what had to be done."

Tears were streaming down his face, and Father Hickey could hear real terror in the man's voice as it pitched higher. "I did nothing wrong, Father. How was I supposed to live?" Ted slumped down in the chair in front of the desk.

Putting his hand on Ted's shoulder, Father Hickey sat on the corner of the desk. "Ted, I am sure this is all just a recurring nightmare," he said in a soft voice. "Your mother is not a demon, Ted."

"No," Ted said, the panic rising in his voice. "But again, she told me Abaddon was coming very soon and I would be called before him to answer for my sins against her." He stood and went back to the window to look at his mother's grave.

"Ted, your mother sounds really ticked off at you," Father Hickey said as he tried to bring the man's focus back. "What is it that she thinks you did, Ted? Why would a mother ask Abaddon to take her child?" He stood next to Ted and looked out the window. Off in the distance, a ferry steamed into port. "Ted, did you hear me?"

"Yes, Father, I heard you. My mother thinks I put her in a nursing home and left her there. But there is more, Father Hickey, much more." Ted began to cry again.

"Ted, I am your priest. You can tell me what it is."

Walking away from the window, Ted said, "My dad died when I was very young. My mother worked night and day to raise me. She never dated, just worked." He sat down in the chair. "I was about fourteen when my mother came into my room one night and told me I was the man of the house now." After weeping for a moment, he continued. "I know now it was wrong. I was fourteen, barely out of seventh grade, and I was now supposed to be the man of the house? I was scared that I would disappoint my mother." He was now sobbing.

"Ted, were you sleeping with your mother?" Father Hickey asked as he sat down at his desk.

Looking up from his hands, Ted said, "I am so ashamed about what I did. What we did." He started to sob again. "Please help me, Father Hickey. Please help me. I am so ashamed of myself. But my mother started it," he said, this time getting angry. "For Christ's sake, I was just fourteen."

"Ted, none of this is your fault," Father Hickey said, sitting back in his chair as he struggled to sort this out. Not one of the classes he had taken at seminary school had prepared him for this. *Not one*, the priest thought. "Ted, have you talked about this with anyone?"

"No, only Father Gilday. My mother was so angry when I got married. She said I betrayed our vows."

"Ted, did you say, 'our vows'?" Father Hickey asked as he leaned closer to hear the man.

"Yes, somewhere along the line, my mother started thinking I was my father, and we were the married couple they used to be. A few times, when we went out for dinner, she would introduce me as her husband."

"After you got married, did things change for your mother?"

"They changed for the worse," Ted replied. "My mother just became a BITCH to my wife. She could not accept that I was married to my wife and not her. All the time, she would call and make up stories that she needed me." Ted was now shaking with rage. Father Hickey knew he had to somehow calm the man down. And quickly.

Trying to bring the man down a notch, the priest said in a soft tone, "It is OK to feel the way you do, but we still need to know why your mother is visiting you in your dreams, Ted."

"Haven't you been listening at all, Father?" Ted yelled. "This is not a dream or nightmare. This is real. For the last two nights, she has been in my home, saying I need to take her back, saying she is sorry. And if I don't, then this Abaddon sprit is coming to drag me and her both down to hell."

Ted stood up and yelled, "Father, I am not going nuts! This is really happening to me! Doesn't she understand that none of this is right?"

"Ted, listen to me," Father Hickey said. "We can get through this. We will get through this. Now, did this ever happen when Father Gilday was alive?"

"Just once," Ted said.

"Good, and how did he take care of it?"

"He came to my home and helped me get her to come back into the graveyard."

"How did he do that?"

"He just asked her."

"And that was all it took? Father Gilday came to your home and asked her to leave?"

"Yes. They were wicked-good friends, and my mother always said she would do anything for Father Gilday. He asked her to come back to the graveyard and sleep until Judgment Day came." Sitting back in his chair, Ted studied the priest for signs that he believed his story.

"I must tell you, Ted," Father Hickey began, "in all my studies, I have yet to hear of spirits coming back to haunt their family. Not to say that this could not or did not happen." The priest lay a hand on the man's shoulder.

"Father, it did, and it is happening to me now. You must believe me." Ted started to weep again. "If Father Gilday were here, he would believe me." He looked right at the priest as tears ran down his face.

"Ted, we need to find the underlying cause of this somehow. And we will. It will just take some time, that's all." Father Hickey sat in the chair next to Ted. "We will need to get you some more professional help. This is something I was not trained in."

"No, I cannot wait to work this out, Father Hickey. My mother will not stop haunting me this time. Don't you see that? Are you not listening to what I have told you at all?" In a panic, Ted stood and headed for the door to the graveyard. Grabbing his jacket, the priest followed him out the door.

The cold morning air stung the priest's nostrils. A seagull screeched in the distance. "Ted, wait! Let's go back in and talk," he said as he tried to catch up with the man walking briskly in front of him. The snow crunched beneath their boots.

Walking through the gate and into the graveyard, Ted yelled at his mother's grave, "You need to leave me alone! I did all I could to make sure you lived a good life! Don't you see?" He stared down at the stone. "I didn't want to put you away in that damn home. I just could not do it anymore. I lost my family over you. My wife and kids left me because of you."

Falling to his knees as if all the life had been drained out of him, Ted softly said, "Now my life is empty and alone because of you. And now you haunt me. After everything I have lost." He started to cry again. "Mother leave me alone. It is time for me to start my own life again. Mother, please stop haunting me!"

Getting back up from the snow, the man turned towards the priest. "I must go, Father. Thanks for listening to me."

Father Hickey stood in front of him, blocking his way to the gate. "Ted, this is a very good first step. We need to confront all the other issues that brought this forward in your mind."

"First step? Father, haven't you heard anything I have said today? My mother is haunting me. Not in my dreams but in real life."

"Ted, I know you believe that, and we can deal with this." The priest placed his hand on Ted's shoulder.

"Ya know, Father Hickey," Ted said as he looked back at the grave, "Father Gilday believed me. He understood everything I said to him."

"Ted. I believe that you believe your mother is coming to your home," Father Hickey said in a quiet tone, "but I have never heard of a spirit taking the shape of a dead parent and coming back to haunt their child. Why would any mother do such a thing?" the priest asked, knowing no answer would follow his question.

"Father, you just don't understand. I came to you for help, and all I got was a lecture on how the mind can play crazy tricks on you in a moment of grief. Father Gilday listened to me and helped me." Ted pushed past the priest and headed out of the graveyard and towards his car.

As the priest watched Ted walk quickly across the frozen snow, he felt a surge of hopelessness come over him. *This is not good*, he thought. Pulling his jacket tight around his neck, Father Hickey walked over to the new, unmarked grave of Father Gilday. He stood there for a moment, not quite sure what to say.

Finally, he said, "Father Gilday, you are well thought of around here. I need your guidance in some matters here that I understand you have had to deal with before. These matters are of great importance, and I am not ready to deal with such pain. I need your years of experience to help Ted deal with the loss of his mother. I ask your spirit for guidance in this matter." After making the sign of the cross, Father Hickey headed back to the warmth of the church.

As the priest walked away, the old man in a black overcoat and gray scarf stood next to the granite cross. Once the young priest had entered the church living quarters, the old man looked out over the ocean and said to the seagull perched on the stone cross, "So, it begins again. I will pray for you, Father Hickey."

The seagull screeched and flew away from the empty graveyard.

CHAPTER 15

As Father Hickey hung his coat up, the phone began to ring. Racing into the office, he answered the phone. "Parish of Saint Peter. Father Hickey speaking. May I help you?"

"Father, this is Janie, down at the Crow's Nest," the voice blurted out.

"Hi, Janie. How are you today?" the priest asked glad, to get some time away from Ted's problem.

"Fine, Father. Thank you for asking. Father, will you be coming down to the Nest today for lunch? Mike asked me to call you and invite you if you were not coming around today."

"Well, I had not given it much thought. It has been rather busy around here already this morning." Father Hickey remembered what Mike had said to him this morning over breakfast. "Yes, I can take some time for lunch. Sure, Janie. Tell Mike I will be down in a couple of hours. If you're not busy afterward, maybe you can show me a bit of the town. It would be nice to see a bit of the seaport, as it seems to be a clear day today."

"Sure, Father, I can do that. Today is slow here, so I am sure Mike will give me a bit of time off to show you around Galilee. I will let him know you will be here in a bit. Good-bye, Father."

Hanging up the phone, Father Hickey headed for the kitchen for a quick cup of coffee, still wondering how he could help Ted Roberts.

"Ahh, enough left for one cup," he said as he picked up the coffee pot. After pouring a cup, he clicked on the television and sat down at the kitchen table. Local news at twelve came on.

"Our top story today is still the weather, but we are also following the story of the double rape and homicide of two women during the night in Tuckertown, Rhode Island. Neighbors who heard the women screaming around two o'clock this morning called the police. When the police entered the home, they found the women dead in the kitchen. Neighbors reported seeing a large man walking away from the house around the time of the murders, but due to the snowstorm, no accurate description could be given of him other than that he was around six foot four, dressed in a plaid jacket and black stocking cap, and was last seen heading down to the seaport of Galilee.

"Residents are asking police if a copycat killer of the fisherman is in town. Police have said they do not believe that this is a copycat killer but just some random act of violence or a home invasion gone terribly wrong. Anyone with any information is asked to call their local police."

Clicking off the television, Father Hickey finished his coffee. Then he picked up the truck keys, grabbed his jacket, and headed out the door to drive into town for lunch and, hopefully, talk to Janie and maybe find out what was bothering her. He thought as he shut the kitchen door behind him.

As he was pulling the truck out onto the main road, he glanced over at the graveyard. An old lady in a dark gray coat, mittens, and a white scarf was sitting on the bench, playing with a small dog. A man in a black overcoat and with white hair waved at the priest as he drove by. Waving back, Father Hickey continued the slow drive into Galilee.

When he pulled the truck into a parking spot next to the Crow's' Nest, Father Hickey was startled as Janie open the passenger-side door and climbed in. "Father, I have some free time now to show you around if you like?"

"Sure, Janie," Father Hickey said. "You are the tour boss. Where shall we begin?"

"Well, Father, the only place worth seeing is Scarborough Beach. It is about fifteen minutes from here. Head back towards the church and go straight on Ocean Road, past the fisherman memorial, instead of taking a right at the stop sign."

Buckling up her seat belt, Janie looked over at the priest. "Tommy, gas is on the right." A smile spread across her face.

"Ok, then, Janie, gas is on the right," the priest said. He backed the truck out of the parking spot and headed down Main Street, out of Galilee.

Standing on the snow-covered sidewalk in front of the Crow's Nest, the bear-man smoked a pipe and watched the truck drive away. "Father Hickey, I pray you can forgive Janie for the sins you are about to hear. And I pray you can help her face the trials of her faith that are coming very soon into her life," he said quietly. Turning back to the bar, the bear-man went inside, away from the cold.

"So, Father, what made you become a priest?" Janie asked as she lit a cigarette.

"Please, Janie, call me Tommy, or Tom if you like. And to answer your question, I am repaying a debt to my grandmother, who raised me. She always wanted me to be a priest. So, here I am, a priest with my first parish. Kinda cool, don't you think? Hey, I am the boss of me and one old cat that I have named Elsa," the priest said with a smile.

"Go straight here, Tommy," Janie said as the priest slowed for the stop sign.

Opening the window, she exhaled her smoke and smiled back at the priest. "Yes, that is cool. Father Gilday would have liked you, I bet." She threw her half-smoked cigarette out the window and closed it. "I really need to stop smoking," she said to no one in particular.

"So, you and Father Gilday were good friends, I hear."

"Yes, he was very kind to me and always had time just to listen." She smiled at the thought. "And he taught me how to play a pretty good game of chess." She looked out the window as the white scenery passed by. "When I needed just to talk, Father Gilday was there to listen." She lit another cigarette and opened the window again.

"Well, hopefully, over time, Janie, you and I will become just as good friends as you and Father Gilday," the priest said as he started through the stop sign. He looked over at the memorial to see if anyone was there today. *Not a soul*, he thought as he continued driving. "So, Janie, how long have you lived in the seaport?"

"Got here October 2001. I could not make ends meet in Boston, so here I am." She threw the cigarette out the window and closed it. "Wish I could stop smoking. I tried a few times, but I just cannot do it. So, any family, Tommy?" She looked at the priest.

"Yeah, I have a little brother, Paul. He is about three years younger than me. And an older brother three years older than me. They both still live in Kansas, where we grew up." Father Hickey slowed the car for traffic as they approached the beach.

"Park over there, Tommy." Janie pointed to an open spot in the parking lot. When he pulled the car into the spot, she jumped out of the car and started walking towards the beach.

The moment he opened the door, Father Hickey could smell the salt in the air and hear the waves crashing against the seawall. He made off in the direction Janie had gone. Coming to the edge of the beach, the priest looked to his left and saw Janie sitting on a bench at the edge of the sand. As he walked towards her, she started to speak, not necessarily to him, almost like to the sea. *Or maybe even to the Lord himself,* the priest thought as he sat down next to her.

"I was on the run when I got here, nowhere to go, nowhere to hide," Janie said as she tried to light a cigarette by cupping it in her hands to shield it from the wind. "Messed up on drugs, messed up on life. Lousy mother, lousy person. Didn't care about nothing or no one." She started to cry. "If it weren't for Father Gilday and Mike, I would be dead now, too." She threw the cigarette into the wind.

A man on the beach was throwing a ball for a large black dog, who would give wild chase at the thought of pleasing his master by bringing back the ball.

"Now Father Gilday is gone. What am I going to do?" Janie cried out in desperation and despair.

"Did you say you are a mother, Janie?" the priest asked. Quiet filled the air; only the sound of the surf answered the priest. "Janie, where is your child?" he asked again.

"I killed my son!" Janie screamed, sobbing into her hands. "I killed my son," she said again, this time in a whisper. "Dear Lord, I killed my beautiful child."

"That is your son buried in the graveyard?" Father Hickey asked, placing his hand on her trembling shoulder.

"Yes. Father Gilday and Mike helped me bury my poor son there."

"Janie, I don't know you that well yet, but I do know from our brief time together that you are a good person who is not capable of murder." Father Hickey turned the woman towards him so he could see her eyes.

"Now, tell me what happened to your son," he said in a quiet tone as he took both of her hands in his.

"My son was born in a no-name town up in Northern Maine. The only thing to do for work there is pick potatoes. That is all I did for ten years, pick those damn potatoes twice a year. When you weren't picking potatoes, you were screwing, drinking, and drugging. I wanted more for my child."

Janie cupped her hands and lit another cigarette. Taking a long puff, she exhaled before continuing.

"When Peter was four, I knew we had to leave. My old man had become more abusive and was now hitting little Peter when he cried. Told me it was for his own good. Would teach him to become a man someday. 'No crying in our home,' he would say." Janie took another long drag of her cigarette. "I was tired of it all. I wanted more. So, one night, I packed Peter and me a bag of clothes and headed to Boston to start a new life."

Janie got up and walked down to the surf. Pulling his jacket tighter around his neck, the priest got up and followed. She stopped just a few feet from the water, and the foam from the waves lapped at her boots. The wind blew her long red hair in every direction. Pulling her hair away from her face, Janie said, "We got to Boston, and he found us there about six months later." She threw her cigarette into the swelling ocean. "He tried to take Peter and me back to Maine." She started to cry again.

"So, we ran again. A friend I had made in Boston told me of Galilee and how it was so out of the way no one would ever look for me here. So, Peter and I boarded the Greyhound bus late one night and came here." Turning, Janie looked at the priest with tears in her eyes. "I came here and killed my beautiful baby boy, Peter. Now he haunts me late at night when I am alone!" Walking past the priest, Janie headed down the beach. The priest kept pace as she continued to talk above the roar of the ocean.

"We had no place to live when we got here. I was desperate, so I moved in with the first guy I met here. I was tired, cold, no money, and lost. My son needed a roof over his head. A bed to sleep in. I was tired of sleeping in bus stations. We just needed a place to stay." Turning away from the priest, Janie continued to talk above the wind. "I took the first place I could find. It did not matter how far I had to sink. I would have done anything for my son." She started to shake uncontrollably.

"Damn, it's so cold!" she screamed, and she hunched against the wind and walked towards the car.

Standing for a moment, Father Hickey looked out over the angry ocean waves crashing at his feet. *Best give her a moment to settle down,* the priest thought. Off in the distance, a few surfers were trying their trade without any luck as, one after another, they fell off their boards in the rough surf. Turning to the car, Father Hickey could see Janie leaning against the hood and smoking once again. Plunging his hands deep into his jacket pockets to keep them warm, the priest started up the beach towards the car.

CHAPTER 16

"So, Tommy, you are not much of a talker. I thought all priests were born talkers," Janie said as the priest approached the car.

"I have found in my short career that it is better to listen. What do you want me to say, Janie?" Father Hickey leaned on the hood of the car next to her.

"Nothing, something, anything." Janie threw her cigarette into the wind. "Did you hear anything I said at all, Tommy?" She began to cry again.

"Janie, I heard everything you said. First, I do not believe you killed your son. I can feel the tenderness in your heart. I can feel the anguish and the pain of your loss. Tell me what happened, Janie. Tell me about your beautiful child. Tell me how your child died and how such a beautiful woman could be haunted late in the night by her son." Father Hickey reached out and touched her hand. "Tell me, Janie. Tell me how all this came to be your burden. Tell me, and we shall share your burden together." He opened the car door for Janie to climb in out of the cold. Shutting the door behind her, he walked briskly around the car and climbed in. J

In a quiet, far-away tone, Janie said, "My poor child was only five years old when he died. When I killed him." She started to sob once again.

"How did it happen?" Father Hickey asked as he reached over and grasped Janie's hand firmly.

"I should have taken better care of him. I was doing drugs at the time and didn't care about anything except my next fix. I was whoring myself out for a fix and a place to sleep. Little Peter was just a nuisance, always in the way. One night, we had some people over to smoke crack, and Peter kept getting in the way, so Malachi locked him out on the back porch, so he'd stop getting in our way.

"The next day, when I came down from my high, I went out back to get Peter, and he was gone." Janie started to shake and sob uncontrollably. "We found him later that day. He had walked off the porch, fallen off the dock, and drowned. I found him washed up on the shore just twenty feet from my bedroom. My poor baby died because I did not care enough to save him. To save him from me." Janie screamed and pounded her fist into her face.

"Janie, Janie," Father Hickey called out, grabbing her wrist to stop the assault on her face. "Janie, listen to me. We can work this out. Together we can get you through this. Together we will get through this." Janie slumped over and continued to sob. "What happened after you found you son, Janie? How did Peter end up in an unmarked grave?" He let go of her wrist.

"When I found my baby, I knew he was dead. I just sat there in the cold water, clutching him, and screaming for God to take me. My poor child, he did not deserve to die because of me. I don't know how long I sat there in the ocean, clutching my child. Father Gilday and Michael came upon Peter and me. They were just taking a walk on the beach when they heard me screaming, they said. They knew Peter was dead right away, so they took my child and me back to the church. Father Gilday gave my child last rites and wrapped him in a small blanket to dry him off. Mike just sat with me and prayed for my child. Later that day, we buried little Peter in the graveyard."

"No one called the authorities?" Father Hickey asked.

"No, Michael said that here in Galilee, we take care of our own. And since it was an accident, there was no need to put me through the pain of all of it again. Besides, Father Gilday said God knew who this child was."

"And why no name on the stone?"

"So, no one would know I was the mother and start to ask questions. That was Father Gilday's idea. He said I did not need to suffer anymore. So, just the three of us knew my child was buried there."

"And what of this man you were dating, this Malachi?" Father Hickey asked as he looked out the front window of his truck, towards the angry sea. The waves crashed against the concrete seawall, sending seawater spraying over the truck.

"He was the fisherman," Janie said as she started to light another cigarette. "I do not know why I am still alive after living with him."

After taking a long drag and blowing the smoke out the window, she continued. "Malachi is the man who was killed in town one night when he was recognized by Maureen as the one who had raped and tried to kill her. The fishermen in town went nuts. They were all drunk anyway." Janie started to shake again, but she continued. "They took Malachi down to the docks, wrapped him in a dragger net, and drug him out to sea behind one of the fishing boats from the fleet." Janie started to cry again.

As Father Hickey stared out the window, he struggled for something to say to the distraught woman. He could feel her looking at him, pleading with him for some sort of help and understanding. "Janie," he said in a soft, even tone, "this is so much for one person to hold inside. The death of your son, murder, rape, and loss of faith."

"I have not lost my faith!" Janie screamed. "I have not lost my faith!" She glared at the priest. "You don't get it, Tommy. I need your help, damn it!" She turned her gaze to the raging ocean.

"Janie, what is it you want me to help you with? What is it I just do not get? What is it I am not hearing?" Father Hickey looked Janie squarely in the eye.

"My son is haunting me!" Janie screamed, and she shook and sobbed uncontrollably. "My poor baby comes to me late at night, crying, begging for my help."

"What sort of help does Peter ask for, Janie?" Father Hickey touched her chin to turn her face towards him.

With tears in her eyes, Janie said, "A few nights ago, I got home late from work." She lit another cigarette before continuing. "I was tired and got undressed and headed upstairs for bed. As I got to the end of the hall, I heard a noise behind me." Starting to tremble again, Janie exhaled a cloud of smoke. "I turned around, and there was my little boy, standing at the top of the stairway. He was all wet and shivering. 'Mommy, I am cold,' he said to me."

"What happened then, Janie? What did you say to your son, Peter?"

Father Hickey asked, knowing it was important to keep Janie talking to get through this.

Janie sobbed like the priest was no longer there and she was reliving the whole scene over like it was the first time. "Peter, how did you so wet, baby? How did you get here?" she asked the ghost in her mind. "Malachi, brought you here? How did you get so wet, baby? Malachi threw you in the ocean and held you underwater? Peter, how could that happen? I am sorry, Peter; I am so sorry. I am sorry, baby. Please believe me!" Janie screamed, and she sobbed into her hands again.

"Janie, did you go to your son? Did you hold him tight and tell him it would be ok?" Father Hickey asked in a quiet tone as he touched her shoulder.

"I tried to," Janie said, sobbing into her hands. "As I started towards my son, Malachi came up the stairs, grabbed him by the hair, and dragged him down the stairs, out the door, and into the night. I could hear my son screaming, 'Help me, Mommy, help me,' as he banged down the stairs. I ran outside, and Malachi was standing there in the snow with my son over his shoulder."

Janie took a moment to catch her breath before continuing. He said that if I ever wanted my son to have peace in death, I was to bring him Maureen and bring her soon. 'Help me, Mommy, help me, Mommy,' my poor baby kept screaming as that monster took him away into the night." Janie began screaming uncontrollably, "Bring back my child! Bring back my child!

Grabbing the woman by both arms, the priest pulled her to him, and she buried her head in his shoulder, sobbing quietly now as if all the fight had left her. Laying a hand on her head, Father Hickey began to pray.

Oh, merciful God,
Take pity on those souls
Who have no particular friends and intercessors
To recommend them to Thee, who,
Either through the negligence of those who are alive
Or through length of time are forgotten
By their friends and by all.
Spare them, O Lord,

And remember Thine own mercy
When others forget to appeal to it.
Let not the souls, which Thou hast created,
Be parted from thee, their Creator.
May the souls of all the faithful departed,
Through the mercy of God, rest in peace.
Amen.

Making the sign of the cross, Father Hickey lifted Janie's head from his shoulder and quietly said, "Janie, I want you to stay at the church tonight. There is something going on, that is for sure." He thought about Ted saying his mother was haunting him and Jackie, the dog, playing with the little girl, Annie, and her husband, Mark.

Nodding, Janie continued to cry. "My poor baby, my poor child. My God, what have I done to cause my child so much pain? Father Hickey, what am I going to do?" she asked as she fought to compose herself.

"Everything will be fine, Janie. We just need to sit down and continue talking you through this." Father Hickey started the truck.

"This is not something I need to talk about," Janie said as she began to cry again. "We need to get my child from that madman Malachi."

"I promise you, Janie, we will sort this all out and help your son's spirit get to God for protection from all this pain and suffering so both of you can find some relief," the priest said in a consoling voice.

"And what of Malachi?" Janie pleaded.

"His spirit needs to head to hell and stay there." Turning the truck around, Father Hickey drove out of the parking lot and headed back to the church.

The ride back to the church was slow and very cold. The truck's heater could not keep up with the cold wind as a new nor'easter was rumbling in off the Atlantic Ocean. Finally, though, they made it back, and Father Hickey said, "Janie, Janie, we are here."

Janie was so emotionally beaten that she had dropped off into a restless sleep during the ride back. Pulling into the garage, Father Hickey got out and came around the truck to help her out. Opening the door, he could see that Janie was still in some sort of shock. It was the middle of the afternoon, and already the sun seemed to be leaving the sky. Father Hickey looked out over the bay—the sun seemed to be sinking into the ocean.

Taking Janie's hand, the priest helped her step down from the truck. "I need to go to the Crow's Nest first," she said.

"The Crow's Nest? Why is that?" Father Hickey asked as he shut the door to the truck. The heat from the day was now gone, and the priest could see his breath in the air as he spoke.

"I need to get some clothes out of my car," Janie said as she started for the kitchen door.

"Well, let me get you settled in, and I will go get it for you if that is ok." The priest opened the door, and Janie stepped inside.

"Yes, that will be fine. I am so tired right now. I just need to sleep. I have not slept for two nights. Thanks, Tommy. If you could do that, I could get some sleep." Janie took off her coat and dropped it on the floor.

"Where do I sleep, Tommy?" she asked as she entered the living room. "Father Gilday always let me sleep in the bed closest to the bathroom." She sat on the couch.

"You have stayed here before?" Father Hickey asked as he hung her coat on the coat rack near the kitchen door.

"Yes, many times. Father Gilday and I would play chess late into the night, and I would crash here instead of driving home so late."

Janie stopped for a moment and looked out the window at the graveyard. "Besides, I was, I am scared to be alone." She started to cry again. "With the death of my son, I became a basket case. Father Gilday never complained. We would stay up until the sun came up if I need to. Lots of times, I would just fall asleep right here, and he would cover me up and watch over me until I awoke in the morning. Did you know him, Tommy?" Janie took her boots off and headed towards the bedroom.

"No, Janie, I never met him. I never knew this place was on the map until last week when I was assigned here. Sadly, when I got here, Father Gilday had already passed away, so I never got the chance to meet him. He sounds like he was a very special friend to you, Janie. I am very sorry for all your loss." Father Hickey picked up the boots and put them by the kitchen door.

Walking into the bedroom, he found Janie fast asleep on the far bed. On the bottom of the bed, Elsa, the cat, was fast asleep, too. Taking the blanket off the other bed, the priest covered the girl and went back to the kitchen.

Putting his jacket on, Father Hickey headed out the back door to the truck for his ride into Galilee. The wind-whipped snow swirled up around him.

As the priest headed into the garage, the old man in the long black coat stood in the graveyard, his hands plunged deep into his pockets to ward off the cold as the wind howled around him.

He watched as Father Hickey drove the truck out of the garage and headed down the street into town. Bending down, the old man patted a small white and black spotted dog on the head. Looking towards the graying sky, the old man made the sign of the cross and headed towards the church.

CHAPTER 17

As he slowed the truck for the stop sign, Father Hickey looked over at the fisherman memorial. In the swirling snow, he saw the big man in the same plaid jacket as the man in the graveyard, standing off to the side of the memorial, smoking a cigarette. Rolling down the window of the truck, Father Hickey called out to the man, "Do you need a ride into town?" The man just stared at the priest. Calling out again, the priest was met by more silence from the man, who continued to smoke. Rolling up the window, Father Hickey lost sight of the man for a moment in the swirling snow. As the snow settled, the man was no longer there.

"Alright," Father Hickey said, "this is getting a bit too weird for me," and he continued his drive into town.

At the memorial, the big man smoked his cigarette as he watched the truck drive away. To his right sat a small boy crying softly for his mother. "Shut up, or I will put you back in the ocean! You will see your mother soon!" the man screamed at the child. He laughed softly to himself as he continued smoking.

In town, Father Hickey pulled his truck into a parking spot next to the Crow's Nest, climbed out, and headed for the bar's door. "Hello, Tommy," came a voice from across the street. Turning, Father Hickey saw Abraham making his way past the slow-moving cars and trucks driving down the slippery street. When Abraham made it to the safety of the sidewalk, he held out his hand. "Good afternoon, Father."

"And the same to you," the priest said, shaking the man's hand.

"Are you here for a late lunch, Father?" Abraham asked, and he opened the door to the Crow's Nest for the priest.

"No, not really," the priest said as he stepped inside the bar.

Shutting the door as he came in, Abraham said, "Oh, just a social visit, I take it, then."

"Tommy, Abraham," Mike called out as he came towards them with both hands outstretched. "Good to see you both today." He gestured towards his favorite table to have a seat.

"So, Tommy, I have Janie's backpack over by the bar when you leave," the bear-man said as he put a beer in front of the priest and Abraham.

"Janie called you, Mike?" asked Father Hickey.

"Yes, she said you would be by."

"How did she sound?"

"Fine, but very tired. She said it had been a tough afternoon and she was just going to sleep at the church tonight. In fact, she said to tell you not to hurry back as she was going to sleep with the fat cat," Mike said with a grin, and Abraham laughed.

"Yes," Father Hickey said with a smile, "that fat cat goes by the name of Elsa, and she does like to sleep a lot."

"So, Tommy, did you and Janie get a chance to talk today?" the bear-man asked before taking a swig of beer.

"Yeah, Mike, we did. Do you know about any of this?" the priest asked, hoping he did so they could talk about it.

"Yes, Abraham and I both have talked to her about it. That is why we asked her to talk to you." Mike nodded towards the other man at the table.

"So, what do you think, Tommy?" Abraham asked, folding his hands on the table as he waited for the priest to answer him.

"Well, I am not sure what to think, guys. I do know that Janie believes that her son is haunting her. And this Malachi person sounds to be totally evil." The priest took a long drink from his beer.

"Malachi? What about him?" Abraham said in a frantic tone.

From the corner of his eye, Father Hickey saw the bear-man set down his beer to listen. "Yes, she said that this fisherman Malachi has her son and is drowning him in the ocean and will not let him rest until he sees Maureen. This nightmare is killing her." Father Hickey took another long drink from his beer. "Mike, this is out of my league. She needs professional help and long-term therapy. It does seem strange, though, almost like some sort of mass hysteria going on in Galilee right now."

"Mass hysteria in Galilee?" Abraham asked, looking at Mike.

"Yes, Mr. Roberts said that his dead mother has been visiting him the last few nights." The priest took a long drink from his beer. "And the little girl Emma says her dead dog, Jackie, is visiting her at night and biting her, according to her mother. Miss Hanson wants to die and go be with her husband, who is haunting her at night. And poor Janie is being haunted not only by the death of her son but also by this killer fisherman, Malachi." He finished his beer.

The bear-man remained quiet, listening intently to the priest.

"But the strangest thing is that Ted's mother says that the chief of the demons of the seventh hierarchy is coming very soon." Pausing to gather his words, the priest said, "She claims that Abaddon is coming very soon."

"Abaddon, coming here?" Abraham said in a panic as he looked at the bear-man. "Mike, did you hear what Tommy said?"

"Yes, yes, I heard what he said, Abraham." Mike passed the priest another beer and leaned forward. "Tommy, are you sure that is what Ted said?"

"Yes, kinda hard not to understand that name, I think." The priest fidgeted with the beer.

"What did you tell him, Father Hickey?" Abraham asked. He looked at the door as it opened, and a group of fishermen came in after a long day of fishing the cold Atlantic Ocean.

"Well, I told him it must all be a bad nightmare and somehow we would get through this," the priest said as he looked at the bear-man.

"But he did not buy that, did he, Tommy?" Mike said as he looked back at the priest.

"No, Mike, he did not." The priest took a drink from his beer. "He told me his mother had visited him the last three nights and she kept crying and saying that Abaddon would be here soon. Now Janie is seeing her son, Peter, with this fisherman named Malachi. Mike, I understand from Janie that you and Father Gilday know what happened to her son."

"Yes, Father Gilday and I came upon Janie on the beach that morning. We found her clutching her dead son in her arms. What did you want us to do, Tommy?" The bear-man put down his beer. "Should we have called the police and put her through that? Should we have judged her that day? It seems she had suffered enough."

"Mike, I am not judging. I am just asking how she has been since then.

Has this ever happened since then?" Father Hickey looked at his watch. "Ted told me his mother came to him before and he and Father Gilday got her to back to the graveyard to sleep until Judgment Day.

"Yes, I remember Father Gilday telling me about that. Never got into much of what happened, just that he helped Ted work out some of his issues with his mother's death. But to the best of my knowledge, Janie has never gone through this before," the bear-man said as he finished his beer.

"Tommy, before I forget, let me give you Janie's clothes," Mike said, and he stood and walked to the kitchen.

"So, Abraham, any ideas on what I should do here?" Father Hickey asked as he finished his beer.

"It seems you do have your hands full right now, Tommy. I suggest you look to prayer for the answers. The Lord is listening and will help you. You just need to ask him, is all. Well, Father, I need to be going before it gets too late. I will see you in the morning for mass." Abraham stood and shook Father Hickey's hand.

"Yes, Abraham, I will see you in the morning. Have a good night." As Father Hickey watched Abraham leave, he could not help but feel that the old man had been holding something back from him.

"Here you go, Tommy," Mike said as he put a small backpack next to the chair the priest was sitting in. "Janie likes to leave a bag her in case she does not get back to her place at night." Sitting down with two more beers, he handed one to the priest. "When Father Gilday was alive, she would stop at the church on her way home to talk with him and play chess. It did not matter to him what time it was. He always had time for a game of chess and to talk. And most times, it got so late she would just spend the night there at the church."

"Mike, who is Maureen?" the priest asked as he took the beer.

"Maureen was the woman who pointed out Malachi the night the townsfolk took matters into their own hands. Kind of mob justice, I guess you could say." Mike looked out the window and watched the snow fall at a rapid clip.

"So, where is Maureen now, Mike?" The priest sipped his beer.

"She works the fleet, on the long hauls. Most of her trips are about a week. Does a lot of crabbing off the shelf. Her boat is supposed to be in tomorrow. She lived with Malachi after Janie and Peter did."

"How did Maureen know that Malachi was the one committing the murders?" the priest asked, leaning forward for the answer.

"Well, it turns out that he made tapes of the murder and rape." Mike took another drink from his beer. "Maureen was cleaning the house one day, and she comes upon the tapes, and after watching them, she calls a few friends of hers she worked with. Well, the mob grew and got drunk, so they went looking for Malachi."

Taking a deep breath, Mike continued. "Well, the mob found him as he was crossing the street out front here. Grabbing him, they dragged him down to the docks and beat him bad. After that, they wrapped him in a dragger net with a bunch of fishing hooks and pulled him behind a fishing boat for a day. A few days later, his body washed up on the beach, pretty much a bloated and beaten mess.

"The local police did not work too hard at trying to find out what happened. They were just glad the case was over. So, a few of the townsfolk took his body up to the church one day and buried him in a shallow grave in the back. Father Gilday was not too happy about it, but the town just wanted this over, so he left the body where it was." Taking a long drink from his beer, Mike looked out the bar window as the snow fell against it and began to stick to the glass pane. "This town has had better days," he mumbled to the air.

"Well, Mike, I think I need to get back to the church before it gets too late. I do not want to leave Janie alone too long right now." Father Hickey stood up from his chair. "Gotta tell you, Mike, that is quite a story you just told me."

"No story, Tommy, just the truth," the bear-man said as he handed the priest the backpack.

"Oh, I believe you, Mike. It's just that…" Struggling for words, the priest looked out the window at the falling snow. "It's just that I—"

"I know, Tommy," the bear-man said, cutting into the young priest's thought. "It is quite a bit to digest after only a few days here at your first parish."

The bear-man paused a moment before continuing. "Tommy, you were picked to come here for a very special reason. In time, it will all come to make sense to you."

"Mike, you are the second person to tell me that I am here for a special reason." The priest held out his hand to the bear-man, and they shook.

"Seems a few people here in Galilee have the same sense about you that I do, Tommy. Tell Janie I will see her tomorrow at church."

"Sure, Mike, I will let her know." The young priest left the bar and headed for his car.

"Good evening, Father Hickey," came a voice from across the street.

The priest pulled his jacket tightly around his neck to ward off the cold as the wind howled around him. Looking over, he saw Mary coming across the snowy street to greet him.

"Father Hickey, I have a present for you, and not a moment too soon, it would seem." She reached into a bag she was carrying.

"And good evening to you, Mary," the priest said as he looked down at the bag. "Boy, is it getting cold out tonight." He stamped his feet for warmth.

"Well, I hope this will keep you a bit warmer on these cold New England winter days."

Opening the bag, Mary pulled out a long, colorful scarf. "This is for you," she said as she put it around the priest's neck and crossed it over his chest.

"Wow," the priest said, looking down at the brightly colored scarf.

"I knitted it myself," Mary said as she tucked the scarf into the priest's jacket. "Now I will not have to watch you shiver so much." She gave the priest a warm hug. "The best gift you can give is a hug. One size fits all, and no one ever minds if you return it. But a scarf is nice, too. So, how are you today, Father?" Mary asked. She picked up her bags and walked over to the door of the Crow's Nest.

Holding the door open, the priest called back above the howl of the wind, "Much warmer now, thanks to you, Mary. This was very kind of you." He touched his new scarf. "I will treasure it always. Thanks again."

"No problem, Father. I could see you needed one, and I like to knit, so it was a perfect match. See you at church." With that, she walked into the warmth of the bar, letting the door close behind her.

Turning back towards the cold night, Father Hickey headed for the warmth of his car.

CHAPTER 18

---◆---

Climbing into the truck, the priest quickly shut the door to ward off the howling wind. "Damn, it is getting colder, if that is possible," the priest said as he started the engine. As he turned the truck down the street, he failed to notice the bear-man and Mary watching him from inside the Crow's Nest, safe from the cold wind howling outside.

"He is so very young, Michael," Mary said. "Do you really think his faith is up to a task such as this?"

The bear-man let out a sigh. "Look how old your son was, Mary, when he started his first ministry." He watched the truck as it disappeared.

"Yes, Michael, and looked what happened to him," Mary said as she turned to head back to the table.

"Time will tell, Mary. It always does. Time will tell." The bear-man turned away from the window.

The road back to the church was quickly becoming a snow path. "So, when do they plow the streets around here?" the priest said to the radio as he tried to find a weather forecast. Coming to the stop sign in front of the fisherman memorial, the priest looked for the figure he had seen there the last few times he had driven past. Seeing no one, the priest went through the intersection and continued his slow drive towards the church.

By the time he pulled the truck into the garage, the priest was glad to be back at the church. *Man, what a day,* he thought. "A dead mother haunting her son. A dead dog that still plays with her little master. A woman who wants to die to be with her husband. And poor Janie," he said. As he looked in the rear-view mirror, a dark shape slowly went by, veiled by the fast-falling snow.

Hmm, the priest thought, *that lighthouse sure plays tricks on the eyes in this snow.* He climbed out of the truck and quickly walked through the snow and up the steps to the kitchen door. Stepping in, he felt the warmth of the room cover his body as he tried to shake off the cold. In the living room, he saw the side door to the graveyard was open and snow was blowing in. Walking over to the door to shut it, the priest stopped as he investigated the graveyard. For a moment, he was sure he was having a horrible nightmare.

"Give me back my son! Give me my son, you bastard!" Janie screamed as she clawed at the face of a huge man in a black and red plaid jacket.

He looks like the man I saw at the memorial the last few nights, the priest thought. Jumping down the stairs, he ran to the woman's aid.

The huge man pushed Janie to the ground and then turned and faced the young priest as he came through the gate and into the graveyard. Father Hickey saw a young child squirming in the man's grasp. His massive right hand was locked around the back of the child's neck. The child was screaming, "Mommy, Mommy, help me! Help me, Mommy!"

"Stop right where you are, priest," the man shouted, and he pointed at Father Hickey.

Ignoring the warning, Father Hickey ran headlong into the man with all the force he could muster. Bouncing off, he fell back with a heavy thud to the snowy ground next to Janie. As he started to get back to his feet for another attack on the man, he was stopped by a kick to his chest. "Stay where you are, priest. I will not tell you again," the man said as he stepped back a few feet from the priest and Janie.

"Give me back my baby!" Janie screamed as she started to stand again.

The man reached down and slapped her across the face, knocking her back to the ground. Scrambling to his feet, the priest once again lunged at the huge man. He grabbed at the man's throat and tried to push him over onto his back. The man pulled back and hit the priest in the chest, knocking him to the ground. The priest fought to regain his breath that had been knocked out of him.

"Now, stay, both of you!" the man shouted at the priest and Janie.

"Mommy, help me, please!" the little boy continued to scream.

"Now, listen to me well, priest, because I am only going to say this once." The man pointed a finger at the priest. "Bring me the sow Maureen, and I will put the child back in his grave. He held the child towards the priest and shouted, "Tell them what I do to you! Tell them!"

"He takes me to the ocean and holds me under the water till I drown."

The huge man laughed. "But since the child is already dead, he cannot die, so he just drowns repeatedly. And if I do not get the sow Maureen, I will drown this brat for all eternity. And there is nothing you or anyone can do about it, priest!"

Before turning to walk away, the man yelled, "Bring me the sow, Maureen! If you ever want this child to know peace, bring me the sow Maureen!" Then he and the child disappeared into the swirling snow. The child continued to cry for his mother until his voice was just a painful echo in the howling wind.

Pulling the sobbing Janie to her feet, the priest walked her to the church. "Janie, we need to call the police right away."

Pushing him away, she screamed, "What are you, crazy? That creep has my son! That creep has my dead son!" She shouted at the woods, "Bring back my son! You just do not get it, do you, Tommy?" She pounded on his chest. "You just don't get it, do you?"

She walked over to Father Gilday's grave. "Father, why have you forsaken me? You told me everything would be alright, that this pain would go. You told me my son would rest until I came for him. And now you are gone, and I am living the sins I have committed. My poor child, why must he suffer because of me?" she screamed at the unmarked grave. She fell to the cold ground and sobbed on the grave.

Father Hickey helped the woman up and slowly walked her back to the church. Standing on the steps of the living quarters, he looked back at the graveyard. As the snow swirled in and around it, he could barely make out what he thought might be a figure wearing a long black coat, standing near the cross. Opening the door, he walked Janie inside. He took one look back at the graveyard but could no longer see anything near the cross, as the snow blocked his view.

Closing the door, he led Janie to the bedroom and lay her down on the bed. He quickly removed her jacket and boots and covered the exhausted woman with a blanket. She cried softly and then rolled over and fell into a deep, dreadful sleep.

As he sat on the bed, the priest had a very hard time trying to put into perspective what had just happened. *This is just not possible*, he thought. Elsa climbed up onto the bed and curled up next to the sleeping woman. Father Hickey stroked the cat's head, and he had to smile just a bit as the old cat purred. *Well, it is good to see someone is happy around here tonight.* Standing, the priest headed to the church for some thought and prayer.

He knelt at the altar, made the sign of the cross, and began to pray.

"O Lord, in this time of need, strengthen me. You are my strength and my shield; You are my refuge and strength, a very present help in trouble. I know, Father, that Your eyes go to and fro throughout the earth to strengthen those whose hearts long for You. The body grows weary, but my hope is in You to renew my strength. I do not fear, for You are with me. I am not dismayed or overwhelmed, for You are my God. I know You will strengthen me and help me, that you will uphold me with Your righteous hand. Even as the shadows of evil cover this woman, I feel the comfort of Your strength, O Lord. Amen."

Making the sign of the cross, the priest stood and looked at the cross that hung above the altar. Then he walked to the second pew and sat down. *Ahh, this feels good*, he said to himself. *It has been so long since I have had a chance just to sit and think.*

"Good evening, Father Hickey," came a voice from the pew behind him. Turning half around, the priest came face to face with the old man in black he had seen before.

"Good evening to you, sir," the priest said in reply. "It is a bit late to be here."

"Later than you think, Father," the old man replied. "How is Janie doing?"

"She is very tired, and I am having a very hard time helping her." Father Hickey noticed a priest's collar around the old man's neck, covered with a scarf to ward off the cold. "I was not aware of another Catholic priest here in Galilee. My name is Father Hickey." He held out his hand.

"Pleased to meet you," the old man said as he took the priest's hand and shook it. "And my name is Father Gilday. You may have heard of me."

As Father Hickey slowly pulled his hand away, he knew from the look in the old man's eyes that this was true. "Father Gilday, how is this possible? I was told you died a few days ago." Father Hickey could feel himself begin to shake. Was it from the cold or just plain tiredness?

"Much has happened to you in the last few days, Father Hickey," the old man said. He came around the pew, stood in front of the altar, and looked up at the cross. Making the sign of the cross, he continued. "None of this should have ever happened, but with you late due to the weather and me…" He stopped for a moment to gather his words. Shaking his head, he continued. "Well, dying before you got here kinda messed things up a bit. But the Lord does work in strange ways, of that I am sure." Father Gilday continued to look at the cross, his hands outstretched as if he were asking the figure on the cross for an answer.

"But why is this happening, Father Gilday?" the young priest asked in a desperate tone.

Turning to face the young priest, Father Gilday took a step towards him. He grabbed the top of the pew and leaned over until he was almost face to face with the sitting priest. "Because you left that damn gate open," he said in a hushed tone as if his words were meant for only the young priest to hear. The old priest sat next to the priest and continued.

CHAPTER 19

$\maltese$

"Years ago, when the poorhouse and hospital were on these grounds, terrible things happened here, things brought forth by ignorance and fear." The old priest hung his head as if to offer a prayer. "The Vatican had quite a mess to clean up here. The pope himself made the decision on who to send. Many of his closest advisors questioned his pick, but he was firm in his decision." Turning his head slowly, the old priest looked out the window at the raging storm and closed his eyes for a moment as if the pain of going on had become his own private nightmare.

"You are talking about Father Tarmey," Father Hickey said as he recalled the stories of the tough Irish priest from his school days at the seminary.

"Yes," the old priest said as he turned back to the altar and bowed his head. The old priest started his story again with a sigh. "Many thought that Father Tarmey as a cure might be worse than the disease itself. He would not shirk from using the darkest of methods to win the battle against evil. But with his victories always came the harshest of prices. To Father Tarmey, the ends always justified the means." The old priest shook his head in disgust. "And the Vatican never cared about the means, just the end."

Standing up as if to ward off the cold, Father Hickey walked over to the altar and stomped his feet as the angry storm howled outside. Turning to the old priest, he asked, "How does any of this concern the thing going on with Janie and her son?"

"Sit down, and I will get to it," Father Gilday said in an angry tone as he motioned to the spot next to him on the pew. "When Father Tarmey arrived here from the Vatican, the church was being used as a school. But not a school in the sense you would think." Father Gilday looked up at the cross as the light from the lighthouse swung past and cast an eerie glow over it. "The school was being used as some sort of macabre test center for new drugs and techniques for the insane and people with tuberculosis and sexual diseases. It was more of a gruesome medical experiment."

Father Gilday began to cry ever so slightly. "Even now, I can feel the pain of all the poor souls who suffered and died here. The walls even now refuse to let the pain leave this building." The old priest stood and walked to the altar, seeking some sort of strength from the figure hanging on the cross.

"As the patients died from these horrible experiments, one after another, they were thrown in a pit outside and covered with dirt and garbage. Since most had no family, there were few questions asked. Just another poor troubled soul who died and left no one to mourn their death or even acknowledged they were ever even here." The old priest wiped away the tears and looked up at the cross for the strength to go on. "Poor Father Tarmey. When he got here, there was no way he could have been prepared for the atrocities that were being committed here."

Father Gilday turned towards the young priest, and the coldness of his breath showed in the hazy light of the lighthouse as it did a slow swing through the window at the front of the church. "Until he got here, Father Tarmey had thought he'd seen all the bad and evil the world had to offer. Well, he was wrong." The old priest took a cigarette from his pocket and lit it.

Blowing a smoke ring towards the ceiling, the old priest continued. "The bishop from Boston brought Father Tarmey down in his carriage, dropped him off out front, wished him well, and drove off in a cloud of dust. Standing there on that warm summer morning, Father Tarmey could hear the screams and prayers for help coming from inside these walls. Evil and wickedness were about to learn fear that day. The fear they were about to learn was one of our Lord's most righteous monsters here on earth."

The old priest took another drag from the cigarette. "Kicking open the door to the church, Father Tarmey announced, 'It is Judgment Day, and hell is waiting for a few of you on this fine morning.'" Shaking even more, the old priest continued as the light from the Point Judith lighthouse found its way into the church through the stained-glass windows and cast an eerie red glow over the cross. "What he found that day was sick children being subjected to the most grotesque experiments. Women naked and shackled to the wall, lying in their own filth, badly beaten. But the real horror had just walked in the door that warm spring morning. The wrath of God himself in the form of one big Irish Catholic priest," the old priest said as he fought the apprehension in his voice.

"'In the name of God, the Almighty Father, I sentence you to hell for the sins you have committed here on this fine day and days before,' Father Tarmey yelled as he walked into the main room. Grabbing the first doctor from behind like a rag doll, he whispered in his ear, 'Judgment Day is upon you.' Grasping the doctor's neck, he snapped it like a twig with his big, bear-like hands. Another doctor attacked Father Tarmey from behind with a scalpel, stabbing him deep in the back. Turning around with a smile, the Irish priest announced, 'It will take more than steel to stop the wrath of God on this day of days.' Grabbing the horrified doctor, he crushed his neck in a blink of an eye."

Sitting down next to Father Hickey with something like a sigh, the old priest waited for a moment. He took a deep breath and then continued with his story. "In all, Father Tarmey sent four doctors on their way to hell that day. Dragging the bodies of the dead doctors outside, he threw them into the pit of trash and wood, saying a prayer for each of their sins. Later that day, Father Tarmey set the pile of bodies and trash ablaze. For days, the blaze continued as he burned everything in the church in an effort to purify after the unspeakable atrocities that had happened in the Lord's house. He even scrubbed the walls with flaming wood to burn the sins committed here out of the stone. Sadly, in his zeal to cleanse the church, Father Tarmey only sealed the evil into the walls. I can feel it even now. All that pain, suffering, and evil. Always trying to get out of the walls, always trying to be reborn."

Catching his breath, Father Gilday took another long drag from his cigarette. He blew the smoke towards the church ceiling and closed his eyes as if he were going to sleep.

Father Hickey was having a hard time understanding the nightmare story he was listening to. Turning to look at the old priest, he said, "Father Gilday, what of the women and children you spoke of? What did Father Tarmey do to the women and children he found in that insane place? Did he kill them, too?" He shook the old priest's shoulder for a response.

"Father, what happened to the children and women that Father Tarmey found in so much pain here?"

Opening his eyes, the old priest continued. "The women and children cowered in a corner as Father Tarmey continued his gruesome task of killing the staff and throwing them in the pit outside. 'Do not fear me,' he called out to the women and children. 'Our Lord has sent me to save you from this terror.' The Irish priest towered over the women and children as they cowered in the corner. 'Blessed are the children,' he said as one of the crying children came over to grab his big Irish hand. 'Do not cry, child. You are safe now. Our Father has sent me to bring you home,' he said to the child.

Wrapping the women and children in blankets, he led them outside to waiting carriages sent by the bishop from Boston. 'Tell the bishop these women and children are Vatican-bound,' he yelled to the priest who was sitting with the driver in the first wagon. 'Also, tell him I will need wagons and places in Boston for two hundred or so by tomorrow. Now, be gone with ya,' the big Irish priest yelled as he slapped the horses into a gallop."

The old priest stood and walked towards the altar, and with his back to Father Hickey, he made the sign of the cross. "During the next four days and nights, the local townsfolk saw an eerie, reddish glow fill the horizon over the church as Father Tarmey continued to purify it and burn down the poorhouses. During the night, he could be seen playing his bagpipes as he walked the church grounds, and the smoke and flames provided a macabre background to his soothing tunes.

"The wagons took all the families from the poorhouses here to Boston and Providence. The women and children he'd first sent off were taken to the Vatican, where they were to live out their lives under the protection of the pope himself."

Taking a deep breath, the old priest glanced out the window as if someone were approaching the church. "My time is short. I must leave now," he said.

"But Father, how do I help Janie? How do I rid her of all this pain and terror?" The young priest rose to block Father Gilday from walking up the aisle.

"It is not just Janie you must help," the old priest snapped back. "It is not your fault, but you have unleashed a great deal of pain as well as death on Galilee these last few days."

"How do I fix all this mess? I do not buy that this is my fault, Father."

"You left the gate open, my son. Now you must get everyone back in and close it to keep them here."

"But how am I supposed to do that?" the young priest asked, looking at the old priest for guidance.

"It will not be easy, Father. The sprits have been out a long time and have tasted the freedom from the hell they have endured here in this graveyard all these years. You must get the ones they seek to lead them back to this graveyard. Only then will Janie and the others have some sort of peace from what haunts them. Sadly, each one of the living has a cross of guilt to bear in all this."

"How can this be the fault of the living, Father?" the young priest shot back as the old priest pushed past him.

Stopping for a moment, the old priest turned around. "And whose fault is it, then, Father? Each has a sad tale, indeed. In Janie's case, she feels the guilt of leaving her child on that porch because Malachi did not want him around that evening. She feels the guilt of being an unwed mother. She feels the guilt of her life." Father Gilday turned once again and headed for the front door of the church. "Each one of them feels guilt over their loss. But Malachi, that one is just pure evil and feels no guilt. He will be the tough one to return to the grave."

"But how will I do this, Father?" the young priest asked as he started to follow the old priest up the aisle towards the front door.

"Bring the living to the graveyard tomorrow night. The dead will follow. I will be there waiting to help you. I am tired," the old priest said as he turned the corner. "I must go now."

"But wait, Father," the young priest called out as he quickened his pace to catch up with the old man. Turning the corner, he was met with a closed and locked church door. As he made his way to the front of the church, Father Hickey mumbled to himself, "On most days, that would seem a bit odd. But not on this day."

Walking quietly into the bedroom, Father Hickey pulled the blanket up over the shoulders of the sleeping woman. *So much pain,* he thought. Elsa had crawled up on the pillows over Janie's head and was quietly sleeping. A soft purring came from the old cat. Walking to the bedroom window, the priest sat down in the rocking chair near the window to think. He looked out over the snow-covered field, but the snow swirled, making it hard to see even the ocean. Off in the distance, he could see the early-morning sun just beginning to rise.

What to do? he thought before dozing off.

CHAPTER 20

The smell of fresh coffee filled the morning air. "Tommy," a voice called out. "Wake up."

Opening his eyes, the young priest saw Janie holding a cup of coffee. "Here ya go, Tommy. This for you," the young woman said as she put the hot cup in his hands. Turning, she looked out the window and started to cry ever so softly while biting her thumb.

"Janie, I know last night was real," the young priest said. He stood next to her and looked out the window as the early-morning sun brought warmth to the room.

The young priest took a sip of his hot java. "I talked with Father Gilday last night."

"Father Gilday?" Janie said as she turned towards the priest. "But how could you do that?"

The priest could see some hope spring into the woman's eyes. "I am not sure how, but he told me what I must do to stop all this madness from happening ever again."

"There is nothing you can do, Tommy," Janie said as she started to cry even harder. "This is to be my punishment for my sins as a horrible mother."

"No, Janie, this is not your fault. I will fix this today, and you will be punished no more. I swear this to you, Janie," Father Hickey said.

"But how? How can you fix this, Tommy?" Janie pleaded. "You saw Malachi last night. For Christ's sake, he is already dead! How do you fight an evil dead man who is torturing my dead son by drowning him every night for the rest of eternity?"

"Easy, easy, Janie," the young priest said in a soft tone. Reaching down, he held her hand. "I need to get them back in the graveyard tonight and shut the gate."

"Oh, just like that, Malachi is going to walk right in there and say, 'Darn, you got me,' as you shut the gate." Her voice dripped with sarcasm. "Tommy, please tell me you have a better plan than that. Please tell me you can do this."

"Good morning, Father Hickey," came a voice from the door. Turning, the young priest saw Rickey standing there in his altar boy suit.

"And good morning to you, Rickey," Father Hickey said as he stepped towards the little boy. "And where might your brother, Glenn, be this morning?" He knelt to be faced to face with Rickey.

"Well, Father, he might be in the church, lighting the candles," Ricky said with a smile.

"Great. How long do I have until mass?" The priest rubbed the boy's head and stood back up.

Rickey made a funny face as he thought. "Well, I say you have about twenty minutes, though folks are starting to arrive now," he finally said, more as a question than a statement.

"Great. Go make sure everything is ready, and say, in fifteen minutes, I will be ready to start.

The young altar boy turned and headed back to the church. "Great. I will make sure everything is ready, Father," he said as he turned and disappeared around the corner.

Father Hickey looked around, but Janie was no longer in the room. "Boy, she is quick. How did she get by without me seeing her? Well, better get ready for services," the young priest mumbled to himself. "I have a long day ahead of me." He reached down to pat Elsa, and she quietly purred at the attention she was getting from the young priest. "A long day, but nothing like the night, I fear," Father Hickey thought aloud as he began to change for morning mass.

"Eternal rest grant unto them, O Lord, and let perpetual light shine upon them. May the souls of the faithful departed, through the mercy of God, rest in peace. Amen. The mass has ended. Please go in peace," Father Hickey said as he lowered his hands and made the sign of the cross.

Looking out over the crowd, he still could not see if Janie was there. Her customary spot next to Michael was occupied by Mary. Walking towards the front of the church, Father Hickey could hear the wind angrily howling outside. Looking down the pews, the young priest thought, *Full house, even in this bad weather. A faithful flock and a full church. I am truly blessed.*

Standing at the door, he was a bit cold today. Each parishioner stopped to talk to the young priest as they did every day. Most days, the leaving took longer than the mass itself. Today was no exception.

"Good morning, Father. Eternal rest. I have always found great comfort in that prayer," Mary said, as she and Michael were the last two to leave the church today.

"Really, Mary? That prayer has always given me great comfort, too," Father Hickey said as he held out his hand to shake hers.

"Yes, Father Hickey, you do have a way of picking out just the prayer to fit the day, it seems," Mary said almost as an afterthought. She looked back at the altar, made the sign of the cross, and turned back to the priest. "Thank you again, Tommy, for such a fine service. And good-bye, Michael," she said as she pushed open the church door and stepped out into the cold morning.

"Yes, Mary, I will see you later for lunch," the bear-man said as he watched the howling

wind slam the church door shut.

"Quite a sermon this cold morning, Tommy," the bear said as he turned back towards the priest.

"Yes, yes, it was, Mike," the priest replied. "Have you seen Janie today?"

"Yes, I have, Tommy. She was at her son's grave when I got here for mass this morning. I asked her if everything was alright, and she just cried and said all her hopes rest with you now, Tommy. Any idea what she meant by that?"

"Yes, I do. Mike, do you know where I can find Maureen?"

"Funny you should ask that. I saw her this morning. Her boat, the *Pandora*, got into port late last night," the bear said as he started to pull on his woolen parka.

"Where can I find her today, Mike?"

"Well, she usually stays with friends across the bay in Jerusalem, but mostly, you can find her on the *Pandora* during the day," the bear said as he zipped up his jacket. Pulling on his hood, he said, "Well, Tommy, I need to get down to the Crow's Nest. Will you be coming down for lunch today?"

The cold Atlantic air rushed into the church. "Yes, of course, Mike. I will see you later today. Tell Janie I will be in to see her," the priest yelled above the roar of the wind.

"I sure hope you can help her, Tommy," the bear-man yelled back. With a wave of his hand, he stepped out and slammed the door shut.

"So, do I...so do I," the young priest said as he turned and walked back down the rows of pews to the living quarters of the church.

Sitting at his office desk, the priest turned on the church computer. While he waited for it to warm up, he took a long drink of his steaming-hot coffee. *Where to start?* he said to himself.

"I hope I am not disturbing you, Father," came a woman's voice from the office door.

Looking up from the computer screen, Father Hickey saw Annie Hanson standing at the door, all bundled up in her parka. "Hi, Annie. No, no, not at all. Please come in and have a seat. Can I get you something to drink?" Standing, the young priest motioned to a chair.

"That is very kind of you, Father, but no thank you. I know you told me it was all some sort of a terrible dream..." She started to cry. "But my Mark came again last night to me at my home. He told me he was so cold and so alone. He told me Abaddon was coming soon to the graveyard to drag some of them off to hell. Please, Father, I cannot take this anymore. I cannot let my Mark be dragged off to hell. Help me! Help my Mark! Please!" she screamed as she started to sob into her hands.

Coming around the desk, Father Hickey knelt in front of the old woman and gently pulled her hands from her face. "Annie, I believe you."

"What did you say," father?" she asked as she lifted her face from her hands. Tears still streamed down her face. "You truly believe me, Father Hickey?"

"Yes, Annie, I really do believe." The priest turned and looked out the window. The snow was falling again, and the gray of the early-morning sky was a sure promise of a storm heading in off the Atlantic Ocean. "I really do believe you, Annie," he said again.

Turning back to her, he added, "Annie, I need you to bring Mark back here to the graveyard tonight."

"Back to the graveyard? But how can I do that? Mark knows this is where all his pain comes from. I will not subject him to this pain again!" Annie screamed as she started to cry again.

"I know this will be hard, but it needs to be done. Annie, if we do not get Mark back here, he will never know peace. Our Lord will come here for him. He must be here when that time comes."

Kneeling in front of the woman, the young priest continued. "Annie, this will be such a hard thing for all of us, but mainly, this burden will fall on you.

Lifting her head and nodding to the priest, the old woman whispered, "What if he will not come?"

"He will, Annie. He will come here if you are here. I know this with all my heart," the priest said in a reassuring, even tone.

Standing, he offered his hand to help her up from the chair. "Annie, now, it is important that you listen to me. Tonight, when Mark comes to you, just leave and tell him you will meet him here at the graveyard. He will follow you and come here." Seeing the fear and such sadness in the old woman's eyes, the priest said, "Annie, when you arrive tonight, Father Gilday might be here at the graveyard."

"Father Gilday?" the old women said in a high-pitched tone.

"Yes, but do not worry. He will be there to help us," Father Hickey said softly.

"Where will you be, Father Hickey?" she asked, wiping away her tears.

"If I am not here when you get here, I will be soon. I need to make sure all the spirits are in the graveyard tonight."

"There are more than just Mark?"

"Yes, sorry to say."

"How many?" Annie asked. She wept as she looked out the window at her husband's grave.

"A few, Annie, a few, but I will make sure this ends tonight. You have my word on it," Father Hickey said, not quite sure how it sounded to the woman.

Turning to the door, the old woman pulled her parka hood tight around her head. "I do not know if I can do this, Father." Looking at the young priest, Annie reached out and grabbed his hand tightly. "I do not know if I can lose my husband again. Let me go with him, Father Hickey." Crying again, she continued. "I have had no one all these years, just Mark and me. I could never have children. Heck, even our dog is gone now. I sit at home, night after night, and pray just to leave this world. I have nothing without my Mark. Let me go with him tonight. I beg you, Father Hickey." Breaking down in tears, the woman bowed her head in pain.

As he looked down at the woman, Father Hickey knew she was right. So many years together and then just to lose her other half was so unfair. The priest almost started to cry from the pain of this woman. "Annie, it is not our Lord's way. When it is your time, it will be your time. Our God works in his own time. But our time here is ever so short, just a blink of an eye compared to the eternal life in Heaven with our Father. Annie, you, and Mark will live again in the arms of our Father in Heaven. I promise you this."

Hugging her, the priest added. "In all my heart and faith, I know this to be true. Annie, you need to be here tonight, and it will be all right."

"Thank you, Father," Annie said as her tears kept falling from her face. "I will try. May God forgive me for doing this, Father." The old lady walked out of the office, her footsteps echoing as she walked across the wooden floor to the door.

My dear Annie, our Lord will and has forgiven you, the priest thought as the women left the church.

CHAPTER 21

---◈---

Looking out the office window, Father Hickey watched as Annie made her way to her husband's grave. he could see her talking to the grave but could not make out what she was saying. Above her, the graying sky promised a bad day. Sitting back down at the computer, Father Hickey started to open the records accounts so he could get the addresses and phone numbers he needed for tonight. While waiting for the information to print, he opened the top drawer to look at the keys on the ring that he had seen before.

"Let's see," the young priest said as he fingered the keys. "A key for the church, an extra set of truck keys, and what could this one be for?" He twisted the jailer-looking key in the air, looking for some sort of lettering. Finally, he put the keys back in the drawer. *When this is over, I will find the lock that key fits*, he thought, and then he grabbed the printed list and his jacket and headed out the door.

Climbing into the truck, Father Hickey could not get those words out of his mind. *Abaddon is coming soon. Chief of the demons of the seventh hierarch., Angel of Death. King of the Locusts. This one has a few names, none of them very good.* As he started to drive, he noticed Emma and her mother waving frantically for him to stop at the front gate of the graveyard, where they were standing. Driving the truck around to the front of the church, he pulled it to a sliding stop on the snow-covered street.

As he climbed out of the truck, he could taste the salt in the cold wind as it whipped around him, trying to knock him down on his way to the graveyard. "Hello, Emma," the priest said as he knelt to face the child. He noticed a wrapped bandage on her hand.

"Jackie bit me," the little girl said as she held out her bandaged hand. Taking it, the priest looked up at her mother.

"Last night," the mother said, and then she took a long drag from a cigarette, "I heard Emma screaming, 'Bad dog, bad dog.' I ran into the room, and there was Jackie, snarling at Emma. Father, it was Jackie. How can this be?" She began to cry.

"It is ok, Mommy. Don't cry," Emma said as she grabbed hold of her mother's hand. "Momma, Jackie didn't mean to bite me." Emma also began to cry.

Picking Emma up, Father Hickey looked at her mother. "I believe you. I believe that you saw Jackie and that she bit Emma. We must get Jackie back to the graveyard tonight."

"No!" screamed Emma. "Jackie doesn't like it here!" She reached for her mother, who took Emma from the priest.

"Emma, it is ok. Father Hickey knows what is best for Jackie. Right, Father?" the woman asked with desperate eyes as she looked over Emma's shoulder at the priest.

"I know this will not be easy, Emma, but it is what needs to be done. Jackie needs to come back and sleep," Father Hickey said in a soft tone. "Emma, it is part of life. Jackie needs to come here and go to Heaven."

The small child turned her head toward the priest. With tears running down her face, she cried, "But Jackie has been bad. She kills cats and bit me. She will not go to Heaven. That's why the dog man killed her." Turning back to the warmth of her mother's shoulder, the child continued to cry softly.

"Please, Father Hickey, help my child. Please help us put an end to this."

Walking over to Jackie's grave, the priest called back, "Emma, come pray with me for your Jackie." Standing by the grave but not looking back, the priest held out his hand. In a moment, he felt the warmth and of the child's grasp. Closing his hand ever so slightly, the priest began to pray.

"Eternal Spirit, we bring You our grief in the loss of Jackie and ask for courage to bear it. We bring You our thanks for Jackie, who lived among us and gave Emma freely of her love. We commit our friend and companion Jackie into Your loving hands. Give Emma eyes to see how Your love embraces all creatures and how every living thing speaks to us of Your love. Amen."

A small tearful voice said, "Amen," along with the priest. Letting go of his hand, the child climbed back onto her mother and continued to cry into her shoulder.

Walking over to the women, the priest rubbed the child's back. "That was very nice, Emma. Now we need to get Jackie back here so our prayer will work."

The small child once again turned to face him. "Jackie will go to heaven?" she asked, her bright red cheeks showing under her hood.

"Yes, child. Jackie shall go when it is her time. Emma, our Lord has no wrath for Jackie, just love," the priest said with a soft smile. "Tonight, when Jackie comes to see you, just come here, and Jackie will follow. Just stand by her grave, and she will come to you." With a sad smile, Father Hickey pushed the hair away from the little girl's face.

"Then what?" the child asked as she fought to stop crying.

"Then we will let Jackie go back to sleep until it is her time to go to Heaven. Emma, she will be fine here. I will visit her every day, talk to her, and make sure she has dog bones. And you can still come and see her," the priest said with a smile.

"Really?" Emma asked, now smiling, too.

"Really," Father Hickey said as he reached out and gave a reassuring squeeze to her hand.

"We will see you tonight, Father Hickey," Emma's mother said as she pulled her daughter tight and turned towards the car. Stopping for a moment, she asked the priest, "Will this work, Father?"

"Yes, I believe this will work," Father Hickey said above the howling wind.

"I hope you're right, for Emma's sake." With that, she turned and headed for her car.

Looking to the darkening sky, Father Hickey pulled his jacket tight around his neck and headed back to his truck. Once inside, he started his drive towards Galilee.

Slowing for the stop sign, Father Hickey looked over towards the fisherman memorial. The heavy snowfall and howling wind made it hard to see. Off to the left, he could just make out a figure standing next to the memorial. Could it be the fisherman? Suddenly a huge plow truck blowing its horn came rumbling through the intersection, forcing Father Hickey to slam on his brakes. "Damn! This is a four-way stop!" the priest yelled at the plow truck as it disappeared down the road. When he looked back at the memorial, the figure had vanished. "This is turning out to be quite a day," he said as he continued towards Galilee.

Driving slowly past the Crow's Nest, the priest could see it was a busy day there. With such a wicked storm coming in from the Atlantic, the fleet would not be going out today. Parking his truck next to the bar, the priest hunched over and started to walk down the street towards the fleet.

"Hello, Father Hickey. I see you are wearing the scarf I knitted you. How is it helping with the cold today?"

Looking up, the priest saw Mary smiling and admiring her handiwork. "Hello, Mary. Yes, the scarf is quite the wind-stopper."

"And very stylish, I might add," Mary said with a smile as she fiddled with the scarf.

"Yes, thank you again for it," the priest said as the wind howled. "Mary, do you know where the fishing boat the *Pandora* is docked?"

"Why, yes, I do. It is four ramps down and second boat on your left," Mary said as she pulled her coat around her neck to help ward off the cold. "Well, Father, I promised I would meet Abraham and Michael for lunch at the Crow's Nest. Will you be there today?" She started to walk away.

"Yes, I will be there in a bit," the priest yelled over the wind, but Mary had already blended in with the crowd, and he could no longer see her.

A moment later, he found the right ramp. "Here we go. Ramp four," he said as he grabbed the rail and started the steep climb down the ramp to the boat docks. "*Pandora*. Well, this must be the boat," he said as he looked down at the words on the back of the boat. The smell of fish was almost overwhelming. The priest started to think back to the dead man he'd blessed when he'd first arrived in Galilee.

"Can I help you?" came a voice from the boat.

Looking up, the priest saw a man on the second level of the boat. "Yes," he called back. "My name is Father Hickey, from the parish of Saint Peter, and I am looking to speak with Maureen if she is here."

"Sure, come on board, Father. First hatch on your left. She is one flight down. Do you need any help?" the man called down over the howling wind.

"No, I am sure I can find her. Thanks, though," the priest yelled back.

As the salty spray hit his lips, he grabbed the rail and climbed awkwardly aboard the rocking boat.

Slamming the hatch behind him, the priest waited a moment for his eyes to adjust to the dim light. The sound of humming machinery quietly filled the oil-stained air. Starting down the stairs, Father Hickey could hear a radio softly playing blues somewhere down below. Stepping into the room, the priest saw a woman sitting at a table with a beer in front of her.

"Bit early for drinking today, Maureen. Don't you think?" the priest said. He walked over to the table and sat next to the woman.

"Father Hickey, Janie said you would be by today," Maureen said without lifting her head.

"Yes, Janie needs your help today," the priest said as the woman took another long drink from her beer. An ashtray full of cigarette butts sat on the table, one still lit.

"Malachi. After all these years, I still have to hear that name. It isn't enough that he haunts me in my sleep every single night." She began to cry. "Sorry, Father, you are wasting your time here. I cannot help you with this." She took a long drag from her cigarette and blew the smoke in the air. "That man was and is just pure evil. It does not surprise me that he is still around. There is nothing I can do to help you, Father Hickey."

"Maureen, I am not asking you to help me. I am asking you to help Janie's child, Peter," the priest said as he went around the table to sit across from the woman. "I am asking you to help put an end to this once and for all. I am asking you to help yourself." He reached across the table and gently took the beer from her hand. "Together, I know we can do this, Maureen."

She looked back at him and continued to cry. "I am so scared, Father. Is he back to make me pay for my sins?"

"Maureen, our Lord will forgive you of your sins. I forgive you for your sins," the priest said in an easy, soft tone.

"What do you want me to do, Father?" she said as she tried to regain her composure.

"I need you to come to the graveyard tonight, Maureen. I need you to be strong so I can make this right."

"But why must I do that?"

"I need to get Malachi back to the graveyard, and he will only come if you are there."

"But how will he know I am there?" Maureen said, terror creeping into her voice.

"I will tell him you are there, and he will come."

"How will you find that animal, Father?"

"I know where the monster lies." He held her hand. "I will find him."

"Father, I do not want to die. I am so scared," Maureen said as she continued to cry.

"Do not cry, Maureen. We have God on our side in this." He smiled at her.

"I do not think I can do this, Father." She lit another cigarette.

"We must end this, Maureen. Don't you see? Malachi needs to be back in the graveyard so he cannot harm anyone else. Janie's son, Peter, should not have to suffer for all eternity. This needs to end tonight, Maureen. Grabbing her hand, the priest waited for a response.

Raising her head, the weeping women looked at the priest and slowly nodded. She whispered, "Come to the graveyard tonight, and I will be there. Together we can end this."

The priest started to leave, and Maureen called after him, "Father ?"

Turning, the priest looked back.

"You can handle this animal Malachi, right? You will not let him hurt me? And you can save poor Peter? You, Father Hickey, can do all of this?"

"Maureen, we have the power of the Lord God on our side. The answer is yes, I can do this with the Lord's help," the priest said, hoping he was right. "You will be there?"

"Yes, Father, no matter how this ends, I will be there."

The priest climbed the stairs and stepped out into the howling wind, shutting the hatch with a clang.

CHAPTER 22

Back on the street, Father Hickey checked his watch: 3:30 and still much to do before nightfall. From the sky, the winter storm was just about to hit the shores. Pulling his jacket tight around his neck, the priest headed back to the Crow's Nest as the wind howled about him and tried to knock him off his feet.

Opening the door to the bar, the priest quickly stepped in, and the wind slammed the door closed behind him. "Tommy, there you are," said Mike, over at his usual table. "Not fit for man nor beast out there today, I fear." He stood to shake the priest's hand.

"You speak the holy truth, Mike." The priest took off his jacket and shook the snow from it. Sitting at the table with Mike were Mary and Abraham.

"Please join us for a bit of lunch," Mary said to the young priest as she motioned to a chair next to her.

"Why, thank you, Mary, I will," Father Hickey said, and he sat in the chair.

"Did you find Maureen with the directions I gave you?" Mary said over the noise of the crowd.

"Yes, yes, I did," the priest said, and he took a beer offered to him by the waitress. Looking at the bear-man, the priest continued. "Mike, have you seen Janie today? I really need to talk with her."

"Yes, Tommy, I talked to her today. She said to tell you she would meet you at the church later today. If you were not there, she would wait until you showed," Mike said, leaning over to make sure the priest could hear him in the noisy room.

"Great, thank you, Mike. How was she today?"

"She seemed to be very upset about something. Called and said she would not be able to work today." Leaning back, the bear-man took a long drink from his beer. "I am worried about her, Tommy. Are you going to be able to help her?"

"Yes, I hope so, Mike. Well, listen. I need to go speak with Ted Roberts. So, I must get going." The priest stood.

"Ted Roberts?" Abraham said above the noise. "I left him about an hour or so ago. He is down painting a summer cottage just outside of town. He does it during the winter to make extra money."

"Great. Saves me from driving in this storm over to Jerusalem. Which cottage is it?" the priest asked as he bent closer to the man to hear the answer.

"Cannot miss it. Right after you leave town, third cottage on your right. You will see his van in the driveway. It says, 'Roberts Painting,' on the side."

Putting on his jacket, the priest began to leave.

"Wait, Father," Mary said, stepping in front of the young priest. "Let me fix your scarf for you. We just lost one priest. We do not want to lose another due to the flu."

Laughing a bit, Mike said, "At least we know he will not be run over in the dark with that scarf on," referring to the many bright colors knitted into the scarf.

Giving the bear-man a "be quiet" look, Mary continued to tuck the scarf into the jacket, and then she kissed the priest on the cheek. "There, all set. Now you will not catch the death of cold."

"Thank you, Mary," the priest said as he turned and headed out into the cold.

After the door shut, Abraham looked at the bear-man and said, "Do you think he will be alright, Mike?"

"I don't know, but his faith is very strong."

"He is so very young, Mike, to face so much," Mary cut in above the noise.

"Yes, but he is all they have now," the bear-man said as he leaned back and puffed on his pipe.

Outside the Crow's Nest, Father Hickey was assaulted again by the salty, icy wind. The streets were nearly empty now. *Quite a difference from an hour ago,* the priest thought as he scrambled to open the door to the truck and climb in and away from the bone-numbing cold. As he started the truck, Father Hickey realized that he was shaking from the cold. He turned the truck heater on high and started the slow drive out of town.

"Let's see, third cottage on the right," the priest said above the roar of the truck heater. The snow was swirling so fast it was a near white-out. "Here we go," the priest said as he pulled in front of the cottage with the van in the snow-covered driveway. Climbing out of the truck, he looked to the sky. Night was falling early; the storm had blotted out the sun. He did not have much time to get this done. Quickly walking up the snow-covered walkway, Father Hickey pounded on the door of the cottage.

"Father Hickey, come in," Ted Roberts said as he opened the door. "Kinda a rough day to be out, Father." He shut the door behind the priest. What brings you here today?" He walked back to a wall covered with a fresh coat of paint.

"Well, Ted, I came to see you," the priest said. Picking up the paintbrush, Ted continued to paint the wall. "Ted, first, I need to apologize to you."

"Really, why is that?" Ted stopped painting and turned to face the priest.

"I did not believe you were seeing your mother. I thought it was just a bad dream. I thought, in time, you would just come to accept the death of your mother and move on with your life." The sound of the howling wind outside filled the room. "But I was wrong, Ted. I was so very wrong." The priest walked towards a window and tried to see through the swirling snow outside.

"You believe me now, Father?" Putting down his paintbrush, Ted sat in a chair, picked up a beer, and started to drink what was left of it. "Why is that Father? Why would you change your mind?"

The priest turned to face him. "These last few days, I have seen and heard things I thought were not possible. I have seen a dead child cry, and I have seen pure evil in the shape of a dead fisherman walk this cold earth. I have talked with a dead priest, and I know what must be done." Almost not believing what he'd just said, the priest continued. "Ted, I need you to go home now and tell your mother to meet you back at the graveyard tonight when she comes to see you."

"Father Gilday did that once, but as you now know, it did not work." Ted stood and walked into the kitchen. Opening the refrigerator, he pulled out a beer and took a long swig from the bottle. Walking back into the room, he picked up the brush.

"You need to trust me on this," the priest said.

"Why? Last time, I cried to you and begged for help. Still, you told me it was in my head." Dropping the brush, the man sat back in the chair.

"I know, Ted, I know, and I was wrong. But you need to help me with this. After tonight, it will be over. Your mother will never haunt you again. Of this, I swear." The priest knelt next to the sitting man.

Ted started to cry. "I never did anything wrong, Father. Why do my fears of did I do enough haunt me? Even if you stop my mother from haunting me, I will be haunted by this forever." He threw the beer bottle against the wall with a crash.

"Ted, I need your help here. Ted, your mother's spirit needs your help. And she needs your help now," the priest said softly as he stood and walked to look out the window again.

After a moment, Ted replied, "Alright, Father, what can I do to help my mother's spirit finally find the peace she is seeking? And Father, what will you do about this Abaddon creature? Mother was very scared that he was coming to take her to the pits of Gehenna. Do you know of this place?" He leaned forward to hear the priest's reply.

"Gehenna, well…" the priest said, struggling to find the right words. "According to some, this is a valley where the idolatrous Jews sacrificed their children to the god Molech. The valley later became the common waste yard for all the refuse of Jerusalem. Here rubbish and the dead bodies of animals and criminals were cast and consumed by a constant fire. Gehenna is cited in the New Testament and in early Christian writing as the final place where the wicked will be punished or destroyed after the resurrection. The name we Catholics have given it is Hell." The priest looked at the tearful man sitting in the chair.

"But my mother is not evil," Ted pleaded with open hands. "Please help my mother, Father Hickey." The man stood up, not sure what to do next, crying for his mother's soul.

Realizing what he had just said, Father Hickey started to feel dizzy. *Abaddon, Gehenna, Hell, the graveyard. Dead spirits tormenting their loved ones. Malachi hunting his last victim to finish the job.* All this started to swirl through his head. The true gravity of what the young priest faced tonight had just hit him.

Trying to shake the dizzy feeling off, Father Hickey looked at Ted. "I will be there with you tonight, Ted, and the spirit of our Lord God will be with us. He will be our strength, Ted. Our faith will get us through this. I promise you," the priest said as he looked the man straight in the eyes. "Our faith will get us through this night."

Looking back at the priest, the man nodded a sad agreement. "Very well, Father. I will go home and wait for my mother. When she comes, I will tell her I am going to church and she can join me there." Picking up his jacket, Ted walked towards the door to leave.

"Ted," the priest called to him. Stopping, the man turned and looked at the priest. Tears streamed down his face. Walking over, the priest put his hand on Ted's shoulder. "We will get through this. I promise you we will get through this."

Ted just turned and headed out the door. A few moments later, the sound of a truck could be heard driving off.

While making sure the lights were off before he left, Father Hickey noticed a crucifix hanging on the wall near the open door. Walking over, he made the sign of the cross and prayed softly to himself as the wind howled in restlessness outside.

"O Lord, in this time of need, strengthen me. You are my strength and my shield; You are my refuge and strength, a very present help in trouble. I know, Father, that Your eyes go to and fro throughout the earth to strengthen those whose hearts long for You. The body grows weary, but my hope is in You to renew my strength."

With tears in his eyes, the priest continued. "I do not fear, for You are with me. I am not dismayed or overwhelmed, for You are my God. I know You will strengthen me and help me, that You will uphold me with your righteous hand. Even as the shadows of enormous evil cover me, I feel the comfort of Your strength, O Lord. Amen."

Making the sign of the cross, Father Hickey closed the door of the home, pushing on it to make sure it was locked. Standing there on the porch for a moment, the priest looked to the sky. Snow continued to fall, creating almost a curtain of white that blocked out the full moon the weatherman had said was there. Looking at his watch, he saw it was six o'clock and night was here. "Time is short," the priest muttered as he pulled his jacket tight and headed for his truck for the drive back to Saint Peter's—and what waited for him and the others.

One more stop to make, he said to himself as he climbed into the truck and started down the street.

CHAPTER 23

Pulling the truck up to the stop sign, the priest peered at the fisherman memorial, but he could not see anyone through the raging storm. He pulled his truck into the barely visible visitors' parking lot, which was now covered in a deep layer of snow. The young priest realized that he was shaking, not from the cold, but from what he was about to do. He climbed out of the truck, made the sign of the cross, and started for the memorial.

The entry to the memorial was nothing more than a carved opening in the stone wall. Stepping in, Father Hickey could hear the slow drip of water as it ran down the walls, freezing on the floor. A single light hung from the ceiling, casting fleeting shadows inside the monument as the power seemed to come and go.

"I knew you would come, priest," came a deep voice from around the corner.

A child's voice came next. "Mister, help me, please! Help me!"

Stepping into the room, Father Hickey saw a little boy. This had to be Peter, Janie's son, all wet and huddled in the corner, trying to be as small as possible, hoping the terror that had brought him here might somehow release him now.

"Peter," the priest called out.

"Yes?" the child replied.

"Priest," came the voice again.

Looking to his right, into the shadows, the priest saw a big man in a plaid jacket and a black stocking cap hunched over on a granite bench, looking right at him. A cigarette dangled from his lips. Pure evil shone in his eyes. Father Hickey knew he had found him—Malachi.

"I have come for the child!" Father Hickey yelled above the roar of the storm.

"I offer him in trade for the sow Maureen," came the icy reply.

"Maureen waits for you at the graveyard, Malachi!" the priest yelled back. He called out to the child, "Peter, come to me."

"Do you take me for a fool, priest?" The smell of fish and death suddenly filled the air around the priest. Turning towards the voice, Father Hickey found Malachi standing right next to him. Malachi grabbed him and lifted him until they were face to face. The smell was overwhelming, and the priest struggled to breathe. "I told you, the sow for the child." Malachi spit in the priest's face and threw him to the floor.

Rolling over, the priest struggled for breath and tried to get to his feet. With a laugh, the fisherman grabbed the priest by the throat again, slapped him across the face, and threw him against the stone wall with a thud. "I will tell you this one last time. The filthy sow for the child!" Malachi yelled at the priest.

Struggling for breath, the priest pulled himself up against the wall. The taste of blood filled his mouth. Turning to face the monster, he yelled, "Maureen is at the graveyard! If you want her, that is where you must go."

Clenching his fist, the priest awaited the next attack from Malachi. Instead, the fisherman laughed and sat back down on the bench. Peter's cries for his mother floated through the cold, stale air. "So, the sow is at the graveyard?" Malachi glared at the priest. "Well, she had better be, or this child you want so much will never know a moment's rest for all eternity."

Walking towards the monster, the priest said a silent prayer. "Malachi give me the child. He is no longer any use to you." He tensed in anticipation of the next attack from the fisherman.

"Sorry, priest, but that is not the way this works." Malachi stood and walked slowly to the priest; his fists clenched. Bracing for the next attack, Father Hickey stood his ground. "The boy and I will go to the graveyard and see if the sow is there." Malachi leaned forward so he was eye level with the priest and their faces just inches apart. The smell of death and rotting flesh filled the air. Malachi's breath smelled of bad fish. "If the sow is not there, I will kill you and torture this boy's soul for all eternity," he said in a low growl.

Walking towards the boy, Malachi turned and looked at Father Hickey.

"Priest," he said with a smile, "have you had Janie yet? Have you tasted the sweetness of her body? Have you had the ride yet, Father?"

Glaring back at the monster, the young priest just said, "Screw you."

Laughing, the monster continued. "That one is so sweet in bed. It is the main reason I did not kill that drug whore. Be rough with her and make her whimper and cry." He grabbed the screaming child by the hair and stormed out the opening in the memorial, dragging the helpless child behind him.

Father Hickey ran to the stone opening, but he was too late. Malachi and the child had disappeared in the now raging snowstorm. Father Hickey could hear the child screaming in the distance. There was not much time. He needed to get back to the church and graveyard. Spitting out a mouthful of blood, the priest raced to his truck.

Moments later, he was pulling the truck to a sliding stop in front of the church. He could see other cars already there and a group of people huddled together in the graveyard. A face appeared at the truck window, and someone frantically knocked on it and pulled open the door so fast the priest nearly fell out.

"Tommy, where have you been?" screamed a frantic Janie. Seeing the blood on the priest, she asked, "What happened to your face, Tommy?" She touched his nose, and he jerked back in pain. "I think it is broken, Tommy." She stepped back to give the priest room to get out of the truck.

"Janie did Maureen show?" the priest asked, slamming the truck door, and heading for the graveyard.

"Yes, she is waiting with the others over there," Janie said as she struggled to keep up with the young priest.

Father Hickey stormed through the gate, and as he approached the group, he counted to himself. There was Emma playing in the snow next to Jackie's grave, unaware of what was about to happen. Her mother hovered over her, knowing what the arrival of the priest meant. Next to them, smoking a cigarette and stomping his feet to stay warm, was Ted Roberts. His voice cracked with fear as he said, "Good evening, Father Hickey."

"Hello," the priest said as he neared the crowd.

"My husband is coming, Father," said Annie, stepping forward from the crowd. "I did just like you said, told him to meet me here. She started to cry as she looked at the gate, knowing that the time to lose her husband again was at hand. Standing in the back, as though hoping not to be seen, stood Maureen.

Father Hickey was not quite sure what to say. Looking at the adults and at little Emma, playing in the snow. Janie had gone to stand next to Maureen. They were holding each other's hands. The priest knew the time had come. Without saying a word, he turned to face the gate. The snow had stopped falling, the wind had calmed down, and the moon peeked out from behind the clouds, casting an eerie glow on the freshly fallen snow.

The priest could see his breath as he exhaled into the cold night. The taste of cold, drying blood filled the back of his throat. Or was it fear? Off in the cold distance, a dog could be heard barking in the night. *So, it begins*, the priest thought. Pulling his old Bible from inside his jacket, he clutched it to his chest for comfort and strength.

"Jackie!" Emma yelled, jumping up out of the snow. "Momma, it is Jackie." The little girl grabbed her mother's arm.

"Yes, baby, I know," the woman said, looking at the gate as she grasped the child's hand.

CHAPTER 24

———— ✠ ————

As the barking drew closer, Father Hickey looked to the grave of Father Gilday. *Great. Fine time for a no-show*, the priest thought. Looking back towards the gate, he saw the small dog he had seen in the graveyard before when all this had started.

"Jackie!" screamed Emma.

Hearing her master's voice, the dog slowly walked over to where Emma stood with her mother. Stepping away from the group, Emma fell to her knees. "Jackie, over here!" the little girl yelled, slapping her hands together. Seeing her master clearly now, the dog ran headlong into the little girl, knocking her back in the snow. Father Hickey could see that the dog was glad to be back with her master. As the dog licked the child's face, Emma's mother stood watch over them, not quite sure what to do.

"Mark, I am over here," Annie called out. As she stepped towards the gate, an old, gray-haired man dressed in a rumpled black suit and gray tie walked slowly into the graveyard.

"Annie, please wait here," the priest said as she struggled to get by him.

"But why? Mark came just like you asked. I need to go to my husband now." The frantic woman pushed past the priest a few steps.

"Annie, please, let's leave here quickly," Mark said as he limped up to his wife. He had a long gash in his right leg.

"Mark, what happens to your leg?" Crying, she looked over at the priest for the help he had promised.

"That bastard fisherman hit me with a shovel yesterday."

"But why would he do that?" she asked, continuing to look at the priest for some sort of help.

"I told that bastard to leave that poor child alone. He just laughed and

130

picked up a shovel he had found and hit me in the leg with it. Told me to get away or he would do it again." The old man reached out and took his wife's hand. "Come on, Annie. We need to leave right now." He tried to make her move, but she didn't budge.

"Mark, we cannot leave." She began to cry again.

"Annie, we need to leave now." Mark back at the gate. The look on his face said that he knew what would soon come through it.

"Ted, where are you?" came a women's voice from just outside the gate. Taking a step forward, Ted stopped and waited. "Ted, where are you?" came the women's voice again.

Looking at the priest, Ted called out, "Mother, I am in here, over by your grave. I need to talk to you. Please come here." Ted's mother appeared at the gate. As she walked into the graveyard, Father Hickey realized it was the same woman he had seen in the graveyard these last few days in the long blue coat.

"Mother, here I am," Ted called out again as he came forward to stand next to Father Hickey. Looking over again at Father Gilday's grave, the young priest began to worry about the absence of the older priest.

"Ted, where have you been?" Ted's mother said as she came up to her son. "Give Momma a kiss, baby."

"No, Mother, it is over," Ted said as he stepped back a bit.

"But why?" his mother asked as she tried to move closer to him.

"I am here, priest!" yelled Malachi from the gate to the graveyard. Little Peter was draped over his shoulder.

Everyone stopped talking and turned towards the gate. "I told you we needed to leave, but now it is too late," Annie's husband said as he looked at the monster there. Jackie turned and growled at the big man.

"Dear God, it is him," Ted's mother said as she stepped behind her son.

"Peter!" yelled Janie as she stepped to the front of the crowd. "You filthy bastard, Malachi, give me back my son!" She charged at the monster.

"Janie, wait!" Father Hickey shouted, but it was too late.

"You want your son? Here!" Malachi said as he lifted the child over his head and threw him to the ground with a thud.

Reaching her son, Janie screamed, "No!" and she knelt by him in the snow, moaning.

Grabbing Janie by the hair, Malachi lifted her up. "Hey, sweetie. Miss me?" the monster said as he kissed her.

"Malachi drop her now!" came a voice from off to the side. "You want me, stupid? Well, here I am!" Maureen screamed at the monster.

"Ahh, the sow. Hmm, which do I want now?" Malachi said with an evil laugh. "The crack whore or the sow whore? I guess I shall have you both." The fisherman threw Janie to the ground and stepped towards Maureen.

The gate to the graveyard clanged shut, the sound echoing throughout the night in the cold air. Turning, Malachi saw Father Gilday standing there with a slight smile on his face. Janie looked up at the old priest and began to cry. Kneeling next to her, Father Gilday said softly to her so Malachi could not hear, "Janie, grab Peter and run to Father Hickey."

"But Father, you are here now to protect us."

"Janie, I cannot protect you for long. Now, do as I say." The priest screamed to Maureen, run now!" and then he stood to face the onslaught as Malachi rushed at him.

Grabbing her child, Janie started to run to Father Hickey, but Malachi knocked her to the ground, grabbed little Peter, and threw him over his shoulder.

Grabbing the old priest by the throat, Malachi lifted him into the air. "So, you think that silly gate can keep me here now?" the monster screamed at Father Gilday as the older priest struggled to free himself.

"Let them go!" Father Hickey yelled as he ran headlong into the fisherman, bouncing off him as before.

Laughing, Malachi threw Father Gilday on top of the younger priest. Then he walked over to the graveyard gate, threw Peter to the ground, and stepping on him. "Do not go anywhere, child," he said, and he grabbed the gate. As the two priests got to their feet, he shouted, "Here is what I think of your precious holy gate!" and he pulled the gate from the stone wall and threw it into the dark.

"Now there is nothing to stop me," he said with a laugh. "Time to collect the rest of my family." He picked Peter back up and threw him over his shoulder.

As he started toward the group in the back of the graveyard, Father

Hickey rushed in front of him. The priest held out his Bible and yelled, "You shall not pass!"

Stopping for a moment, Malachi just laughed. "Priest, I think I will just kill you now so, for all eternity, I will have you to kick around." He stepped forward to grab the priest.

Clutching his Bible to his chest, Father Hickey prayed, "God, with Your great wisdom, You direct the ministry of Angels and men. Grant that those who always minister to You in Heaven may defend us during our life here on earth. Amen." Then, in defiance of what was charging towards him, he added," Also, Lord, I really wish You would just kick this guy's ass. Amen." Making a fist, the priest prepared to defend himself.

"Malachi!" someone shouted.

Stopping short just inches of the priest, the monster turned toward the voice. Looking over, Father Hickey saw a man with long red hair in a long black trench coat. The man had his hands in his pockets.

"What did you say to me?" Malachi said as he took a step towards the man.

"If I were you, I would be treasuring my last few moments here on this earth," the man said as he took a step forward. "Even now, he comes for you. If I were you, I would not waste my time threatening women and children. I would be enjoying these last few moments I have here on this fine night." Looking right at Malachi, the man said, "He is here now," and he looked to his right. There stood a man in a long black hooded robe.

"What are these parlor tricks, priest?" Malachi yelled back at Father Hickey.

"Malachi look at me," hissed the man in the long black hooded robe.

As the man as pulled back his hood, Malachi screamed, "No! No, it cannot be!" He dropped Peter to the ground.

"Yes, my dear friend, it is I, your new master."

Father Hickey could not believe his eyes. The man had the head of a giant locust.

"Child, come to me, quickly," the man in the long coat said as he motioned for Peter to come to him. Getting up, Peter ran to the man and stood behind him. After a moment, the child stuck his head around the man and waved and yelled to his mother, "I am alright, Mommy, really."

The child is now safe, Father Hickey thought with a sigh of relief. *Whoever this man is, right now, Malachi has bigger problems than little Peter.*

Father Gilday walked up to stand next to the young priest. Father Hickey said, "Who is that man, Father Gilday?"

The old priest said just three words: "Gabriel the archangel."

"So, Gabriel, we meet again," the man with the locust head hissed.

"It has been a long time, Abaddon."

"It would seem you survived our last meeting. As I recall, it was not too pleasant for you, Gabriel," Abaddon hissed.

"Well, demon, things change."

At that moment, Malachi tried to run from the creature. "Not today, Malachi. I have waited too long for you, my most cherished prize!" Abaddon yelled as he reached into his robe and came out with a whip. He snapped it at Malachi, and it wrapped around his neck, bringing him to the ground with a painful thud. He pulled Malachi back. "If you try that again, creature, we shall just get an early start on all of eternity for you," Abaddon said As Malachi lay there, trying to catch his breath at the feet of his new master.

"This was a long trip for me to make to collect just this one soul," Abaddon hissed as he looked over to the crowd of people standing over in the corner of the snowy graveyard. "While I am here, I will collect the rest of the dead souls and take them with me now."

"No!" screamed Annie. "You cannot take my Mark! I will not let you!"

"You are not taking my son!" Janie screamed as she stepped forward.

Abaddon screeched, "Do you really think you can stop me?" and he stepped toward the crowd.

"No, but I can!" Gabriel yelled as he threw open his jacket to reveal a long sword at his side, bringing Abaddon to a stop just inches from the two priests.

The demon spun to face the man. "So, you think you can stop me, angel? Last time, you did not fare so well, as I remember." With a hiss, the demon stepped towards Gabriel, his whip out and ready in his hand.

"Like I said before," Gabriel said, drawing the sword and pointing it at the demon, "times have changed."

CHAPTER 25

---✦---

"I am not worried about my little brother," a familiar voice echoed from the gate of the graveyard, "but let's just keep this with the older folks." Mike stepped into the light.

Taking a step back, Abaddon hissed, "So, it is the ugly brother."

"Hey, bug, missed you, too," Mike said with a smile as he walked into the graveyard, a huge ax in his hand.

"I see you still use the battle-ax, brother," Gabriel said as Mike stood next to him.

"Yes, I still favor it," Mike said. "It has always done a good job of cutting off locust heads." He looked at Abaddon. He was referring to the locust plague that nearly consumed Ireland many years ago. God had sent Michael and Gabriel to stop it, and they did when Michael cut Abaddon's head off.

"I see you still remember this ax," Mike called out, and Abaddon clutched his neck, remembering the pain of his last encounter with it. "Get on with your business, bug, before we make you our business." Brandishing his ax, Mike took a step towards Abaddon. Gabriel stepped forward with him. Taking a step back, the creature put away his whip.

"Very well," Abaddon said. He bent down and picked up Malachi by the back of his neck, dragging him to his feet.

"Do not look, child," Gabriel said as he pulled little Peter closer to him. The child turned his face away from what was about to happen.

"I can smell you fear even now. I can taste it," Abaddon said as he quickly licked the back of Malachi's neck. He hissed. "I have waited so long for a prize such as you. For too long, I have had no one as worthy as you to grace my part of Gehenna. You are, indeed, to become my favorite."

Malachi was frozen with fear. He tried to scream but could not.

"Well, it is time to go. Say good-bye to everyone." Abaddon laughed as he picked up the fisherman's hand and waved it in the air. He twisted Malachi's head slightly around to look into his eyes. The demon could see the man's fear all the way into his soul. "Your suffering will be legendry," Abaddon whispered as he pressed his claws into Malachi's back, "even in Hell."

Abaddon wrapped his claws around the fisherman's spine and lifted him over his head like a rag doll. As Abaddon slowly walked off into the night, laughing, Malachi screamed for forgiveness. After a moment, the screams faded away.

"Well, it would seem Malachi is on his way to his new home," Gabriel said. He turned towards Michael with a smile. "It is good to see you again, big brother." He put a hand on Mike's shoulder.

Grabbing Gabriel in a bear hug, Mike replied, "And the same to you, little brother."

Letting go of each other, the two archangels walked over to the two priests, with little Peter in tow.

"It is good to see you again, Michael," Father Gilday said as he hugged the bear-man.

"Ahh, and it is good to see you also, Father."

"Quite a prayer, Father Hickey," Gabriel said as he stood in front of the young priest.

Bowing his head, Father Hickey knelt in front of the archangels. "Hold on, Tommy," Mike said, and he grabbed the priest by his shoulder. "Stand up, Tommy. You are going to embarrass me," he said with a bit of a laugh.

As the young priest stood back up, he was pretty sure this was just a dream. "No, Father Hickey, this is no dream," Gabriel said. He knelt next to Peter. "Peter, go say good-bye to your mother. We must leave soon to go home."

"Home?" the child said.

"Yes, child, back to our Father. Now, go to your mother, child." Gabriel turned little Peter in the direction of his mother, and with a little push, the boy ran to her.

"Mommy," Peter called as he raced headlong into Janie's open arms.

"I really wish you would just kick this guy's ass. Amen," Gabriel said to his brother Michael with a laugh.

"What do you think, Father Gilday? New Testament," Mike said. Shaking his head, he began to laugh.

"Must be something new they teach the kids in school," Father Gilday said as he walked over to Janie and her child.

"Michael, my time is near. I must get ready to go," Gabriel said as he walked over to Emma and her dog, Jackie. Kneeling to face the girl, the angel smiled. "Hello, Emma. My name is Gabriel. I work in Heaven."

"Hello," Emma said as she pulled her dog closer to her.

"I am not going to hurt Jackie, Emma."

"You're not?"

"No, child, God has no wrath for your dog. But Jackie must sleep here for now."

"Why?" Emma said, and she started to cry. "I want Jackie to go to Heaven."

"Jackie shall go to Heaven," the angel said as he wiped away the child's tears with his hand.

"She will?" The child looked up into Gabriel's eyes.

"Yes, child. Many years from now, when it is your turn to come home, you will stop here to get Jackie and take her to Heaven with you," The angel said with a smile. "Jackie is truly your dog, and I do not believe she would be happy unless you are always with her. So, Jackie will sleep here until you come to get her." After patting the dog on the head, the archangel stood.

Turning to her master, Jackie gave Emma a big lick on the face. Then she walked over to her grave, lay down, and slowly disappeared into the snowy ground.

Emma's mother picked the silently crying child up and walked towards the gate. She stopped next to Father Hickey. "Thank you for everything, Father."

"Remember, dog bones every day," Emma said.

"Yes, Emma, dog bones and red balls every day. I promise," the young priest called to the child, and then they walked out the gate and out of sight of the priest.

"Maureen," Gabriel called. Stepping through the group of people, Maureen came forward, and she stopped just short of the guardian angel.

137

"Child, Malachi shall haunt you no more." Gabriel leaned forward and placed a hand on the woman's shoulder.

"But I have done so much wrong in my life." Maureen started to shake and cry. "I do not want that creature to come for me one day."

"Child, you are absolved of all your sins. What you do with the rest of your time here will decide who comes for you in the night. Beware. This is not a pass, but a new beginning. How you live your life now will decide how you live for all eternity. Maureen, it is not hard to live a good life." The angel smiled. "Be good, child." He stepped aside so Maureen could leave the graveyard. Looking back at Janie with a smile, the woman turned and left the graveyard.

Gabriel walked over to where Ted and his mother stood hand in hand, fearing what might come. "Much has happened here. Our Lord is not happy with either of you, but he does forgive you," the archangel said as he looked at the mother and son. "Father Hickey," he called.

"Yes, my lord?" the young priest said as he took a step forward.

"This man here will confess all his sins to you. You will then absolve him of them and guide him in his spiritual life." Looking back at Ted, he said, "You will be given a new lease on your soul. Use it well." He smiled as he touched the man's shoulder.

Turning towards the woman, the archangel Gabriel scowled. "You have much to answer for, Susan. What you did to your poor child will be very hard to forgive. But given the pain you have suffered here; our Lord has told me to bring you with me to be with him." Gabriel smiled. "This is rightfully a great day for you, Susan. You will truly find peace for you soul now."

"Janie, it is time," Michael said quietly. He knelt next to the woman as she clutched her son to her body. "Peter is finally safe and will find peace with his Father. This is the most joyful time for your son." His eyes welled with tears.

"But I can't let go," the woman cried as she pulled her child tighter to her body.

"Janie, it is alright. It is Peter's time." Michael touched the woman's shoulder. "My brother will watch over your son now, Janie. This, I promise you." He touched the child's head.

"Mark," Gabriel said with a smile, "I have long wanted to meet you.

Your life has been one of great faith and good." Smiling, the archangel touched Mark's shoulder.

"I need to stay with my wife. She is alone now, and I cannot leave her here by herself," Mark said as he held his wife's hand and cried.

"Gabriel, my lord," Father Hickey said as he stood next to the angel.

Turning to the priest, the archangel smiled and nodded. Then he looked back at Annie and smiled. "Annie," Father Hickey has told me it is your time. As he reached out to touch Annie's shoulder, she took his hand and kissed it.

"Thank you, my lord." To Father Hickey, with tears in her eyes, she whispered, "Thank you, Father."

"Father Gilday," Gabriel said as he turned towards the priest, "it is not your time yet. Our Lord has asked that you stay a bit longer as there is still much to do."

"I understand," Father Gilday said. He walked towards his grave.

"Father Gilday, wait," Father Hickey called, and he went over to the other priest.

"It is ok, son. I knew it was not my time just yet," the old priest said with a smile as he held Father Hickey's hand. "My son, there is still much you do not know here, but I will be here when you need me." He smiled. "Can you do me a favor, though?"

"Anything, Father," the young priest said.

"Just give me a simple stone, please, so folks can find me when they come to visit." The old priest slowly started to disappear.

"Consider it done," Father Hickey said with a smile. Then the old priest's hand was gone from his grasp.

Gabriel stepped back from the crowd and said to Michael, "It is time for me to leave, brother."

"Come, Janie. It is time," Michael said as he helped the woman to her feet. As she walked slowly towards Gabriel, holding Peter's hand, she continued to cry.

"It is time to go, everyone," the archangel called again.

"Good-bye, mother. I am so sorry for everything," Ted said as he hugged his mother.

"I will always love you," she replied, stopping for a moment to kiss him on the cheek, "son."

Holding each other's hands, Mark and Annie walked towards the archangel. Stopping for a moment, Annie reached over and kissed Father Hickey on the cheek. Then she continued with her husband.

"It has been good to see you again, Michael. Father sends his best and knows you are well," Gabriel said with a smile as he hugged his brother.

"Same, little brother. Tell Father I will be home to visit soon," the bear-man said as he stepped back. "Be well, Gabriel."

"Father Hickey, you have done well," said Gabriel. "Your faith is very strong. But you have yet to learn why our Lord sent you here."

"Why was I sent here, my lord?" Father Hickey asked as he stepped forward.

"In time, Father. In time."

Reaching down, Gabriel held out his hand to Peter. The child took the archangel's hand and walked with him as the others followed. "Bye, Mommy. I will see you soon," Peter called back to his mother.

Helping Janie up from the ground, Father Hickey held her hand as they watched the group walk away.

"Mister?" the small boy said.

"Yes, child," Gabriel replied.

"Do they have dogs in Heaven?" Peter asked, looking up at the angel as they walked.

"Why, yes, they do, Peter."

"Do you think I could have a puppy of my own?"

"Hmm, I do not see why not. There are many puppies in Heaven who would love a boy such as you," Gabriel said with a laugh and smile. "Why, I have several dogs myself, Peter. I am sure we can find one for you."

"Wow!" Peter said, excitement filling his voice.

"You know, Peter, I think dogs are one of our Father's greatest creations," Gabriel said as they started to disappear into the early-morning light.

"Heaven sounds great."

"It is child. It is," softy came the reply.

CHAPTER 26

✢

The early-morning sun was just starting to show on the horizon when Mrs. Szymanowska brought two cups of coffee to the two rocking chairs on the side porch off the living quarters. Michael had started a fire in the old wood stove, and its warmth had almost melted the cold away from the porch. "Here ya go, Father Hickey. Just the way you like it, light with two sugars. And Michael, black with just a bit of Irish whiskey for your cold."

"Mrs. Szymanowska, you remembered," Father Hickey said with a smile as he took the hot cup from the housekeeper.

"Of course, Father. You are the head of this parish now. You have earned your coffee the way you want it. And you, Michael," she turned to the other priest, "are just so damn ugly. How can I say no?"

"True enough, Maria. Gabriel did get all the looks in our family," Michael said, smiling as he took his cup of hot joe.

As she turned and headed back inside, Maria called back, "Well, if you need me, I will be cleaning and making breakfast."

Taking a sip of the hot coffee, Father Hickey looked out over the graveyard and thought about the last few nights. Was it all a dream?

"No, Tommy, it was not a dream," Michael said, interrupting the young priest's thoughts.

"I know," Father Hickey said, sipping his coffee. "I know this was not a dream. I am sitting here with St. Michael the Archangel. You are one of our Lord's most precious—"

"Hold on, Tommy. Our Father loves us all equally. We are all his children." Michael reached over and touched the young priest's shoulder.

"Yes, but you, my lord—"

"Hold on again there, Tommy." Michael put his hand up. "You have come to know me as Mike, a local bar owner here in Galilee. I would like to keep our friendship that way." He turned back to look at the sunrise. "I have been here many years in Galilee as a guardian angel for many people from our past.

"Our past?" Father Hickey said as he leaned forward in his chair and closer to the angel.

"Yes, our past. Many people from the Bible have chosen to make their home across the harbor in Jerusalem. Why, Tommy, you have met the twelve apostles." Michael leaned toward the young priest. "You have been hugged by Mary, the earthly mother of our Savior. Heck, Tommy, she knitted you that scarf around your neck. You still do not see it, do you?" The guardian angel looked out across the graveyard, towards the ocean.

"Our Lord chose you for this place to shepherd the most faithful of his flock, to be the guardian of the faith that has held us together these so many years. Tommy, sometimes the Lord's Son will sit in on your services. Heck, he already sat in on one of your sermons," the bear-man said with a smile.

"Our Savior sat in on one of my services?" Father Hickey said.

"True enough, Tommy. He did. He will often come to Galilee to stay for a bit and visit with his mother, Mary." The bear-man laughed. "Heck, Mary even knitted the Savior His own scarf."

Looking towards the living quarters, the young priest started to get out of his rocking chair.

"Leave her be. She needs her sleep," Michael said as he watched a car drive up to the church. "Janie will recover in her own time. It is important that you be here for her when she needs you, Tommy."

"And me, Mike?" the priest said as he looked at the archangel. "Michael, what is my purpose here? Why did our Lord pick me for such a great honor as a shepherd for His most faithful?"

The car stopped in front of the walkway, and with a slight smile, Michael said, "Look at that. Well, Tommy, it would appear your answer is here." He pointed at the man as climbing out of the car. Getting out of his rocker, Mike looked at the church. "Tommy, you may not know it, but you have been given a very tough job." He held up his hand to stop the priest from talking. "Tommy, it will all become clear in a moment." He watched the man from the car walk towards them.

"Tell Janie I will see her tomorrow at services. No need for her to work today," Michael said to Father Hickey. "May the lord bless you, Tommy. Ahem.." The bear-man touched the priest's forehead and made the sign of the cross. Turning, walked down the stairs towards the man. Stopping for a moment, the man bent over and kissed Michael's hand. Then he continued up the walkway towards Father Hickey.

"Good day, Father Hickey," the man said as he held out his hand. "I am Bishop Flaherty."

"Pleased to me you, Bishop," the young priest said, taking the bishop's hand and kissing his ring.

"I see you have met Michael," the bishop said as he watched the archangel climb into his truck and drive away with a toot of the horn.

"Yes, I have. As far as archangels go, I think he is a nice one," Father Hickey said with a smile.

"Come, we have much to do, and my time is short," the bishop said as he walked by the priest and into the living quarters.

In the office, Bishop Flaherty opened the top drawer, pulled out the jailer-like keys, and held them up for Father Hickey to see. "Father, these are very important keys. You must always know where they are. Never lose them." The bishop left the office, and Father Hickey followed close behind. "These keys, Father Hickey, are your reason for being here." The bishop opened the door to the church hall.

Kneeling at the altar, the bishop quickly said a prayer, and then Father Hickey said one as well. Walking to the wall to the left of the altar, the bishop pushed the key into a small crack in the stone. "This is where the key goes, Father Hickey." He stepped back so the priest could see where he had put the key. "The lock is in the crack, so you must make sure the key is pushed in slowly until you hear the click." At the sound of a click, the bishop pushed the wall, and it slid back into darkness.

"Bishop, what is this?" Father Hickey asked as the bishop flicked a light switch on the other side of the wall, illuminating wooden stairs that went down below the church.

"Why you are here, my son." The bishop started down the stairs. "Come, Father Hickey," he called.

At the bottom of the stairs was a cellar like any other. The bishop was standing by a heavy metal door on the other side of the room. "This is why you are here, Father Hickey." He motioned for the young priest to come near. Reaching up, he pulled open a small window in the door.

Walking up to look through it, Father Hickey could smell burning flesh and something else…something hideous. Gasping for breath, he choked out the words, "Oh…my…God.

Slamming the door shut, the bishop said, "No, not God."

Lightning Source UK Ltd.
Milton Keynes UK
UKHW011942080321
380016UK00012B/1692/J